WINTER VISION

Geoff Page grew up in Grafton and Armidale and was educated at the University of New England. He has taught at high schools in Canberra where he has lived since 1964. His poems have been widely published since the 1960s and he is the author of eight collections of poetry. He has also had several plays and radio features broadcast. He has been the recipient of Literature Board grants and was writer-in-residence at Wollongong University (1982) and at the Australian Defence Force Academy (1987). His first novel, *Benton's Conviction*, was shortlisted for the *Age* Book of the Year Award (1985).

Married with one son, he is currently senior teacher of English at Narrabundah College. Geoff Page is also well known as a literary reviewer.

By the same author

poetry

The Question (in Two Poets, with Philip Roberts)
Smalltown Memorials
Collecting the Weather
Cassandra Paddocks
Clairvoyant in Autumn
Collected Lives
Smiling in English, Smoking in French
Footwork

fiction

Benton's Conviction

translation

Century of Clouds: Selected Poems of Guillaume
    Apollinaire (with Wendy Coutts)

as editor

Shadows from Wire: Poems and Photographs of
    Australians in the Great War

WINTER VISION

GEOFF PAGE

University of Queensland Press

First published 1989 by University of Queensland Press
Box 42, St Lucia, Queensland 4067 Australia

Typeset by University of Queensland Press
Printed in Australia by The Book Printer, Melbourne

Distributed in the USA and Canada by
International Specialized Book Services, Inc.,
5602 N.E. Hassalo Street, Portland, Oregon 97213-3640

Creative writing program assisted by
the Literature Board of the Australia
Council, the Federal Government's arts
funding and advisory body

Cataloguing in Publication Data

National Library of Australia

Page, Geoff, 1940–
    Winter vision.

    I. Title.

A823'.3

ISBN 0 7022 2239 9

Acknowledgments

I would like to thank both the Literature Board of the Australia Council and the English department of the Australian Defence Force Academy for a period as writer-in-residence during which a substantial part of this novel was written. Thanks also are due to Dr Hugh Smith of ADFA and Alan Gould for valuable suggestions on earlier drafts.

1

It was one of those late afternoon gigs at the Yacht Club. Fifty bucks each plus drinks. Roydon Porter, as his brushes flicked and whispered across the snare, glanced out sideways at the turbid water enamelled now by the western sun. High behind the hospital the sides of Black Mountain, the stems of pale gums, were caught in the same light and a few last triangular silhouettes sailed low down in the frame of the full-length window. The clarinetist was taking two choruses of "Georgia On My Mind". That ebony low-register sound was often the only thing left in this music that could still shiver the skin on Roy's neck. It was doing that now, helped by a slight looseness of light ale, just enough to smooth the edges. He looked out over the audience, the tables and jugs of beer, the men tipped back a little in their chairs, the women with a shine in their eyes, singing the lyrics to themselves ("The same sweet sound as moonlight through the pines"). At the bar, Roy noticed, the men who most of the time had their backs to the music had turned around now as if to check the tension, a space in the room they could not explain.

The clarinetist was on his last eight now, skating the

heights of the upper register, while Jake shook the spit from his horn and stood ready for his run up to the first note of the final chorus. The nostalgia in the room was almost tangible, bouncing off the glass, rising from the tables, from the pools of slopped beer, spreading out sideways over the lake and into the late golden light. A nostalgia, Roy would reflect later as he packed up his drums, which few, if any, of them had any right to. Broadway in the twenties, the Harlem dance halls, the Chicago bootleg parlours could not be personal memories for anyone in the room. Nostalgia, he knew, was a continuum, and its object always the same. It was impossible to imagine when trad had not been nostalgia. Maybe even in the twenties it was looking backwards over its shoulder as Louis Armstrong dragged it forward unaware towards the flowing fours of swing and the dizzy technicalities of bop.

On the last held chord Ray went into one of his simpler fills, finishing on an open cymbal and leaving its sound to hang in the air and be overwhelmed by clapping bouncing off the glass and ceiling and whistles that went on up from where the clarinet left off. Jake, the cornetist, went straight on, not waiting for it to die. He called "Found a New Baby" to the pianist and turning back to face the audience stamped down hard with his right foot. "One . . . two . . . one two three four."

Even kicking along at 120 a minute Roy found his mind would wander a little. Much of it was instinctive now: the fill at the end of every eight, the pushing in under the soloist, the scattered accents to fill the gaps, the two bar roll to launch a new solo; also that need not to go with the rush, to keep the time precisely from that first hard foot down on the floor. Roy Porter might be short on chops but he kept good time, you had to give him that. There were others who couldn't.

The irony in the title, even in the chords, didn't worry him now the way it might once have done. It had been quite a while since Roy Porter had "found a new baby". There'd been a couple of "close encounters", as he thought of them later, just after the divorce, but that had been at the height of the AIDS scare which had put everything like that into permanent slow motion. He'd grilled his own chicken seven years now. At fifty-five with thinning hair and a little paunch a "new baby" would probably take more effort than he really wanted to make. There were things about an empty house and a good sound system that were, finally, satisfactory. He looked out over the half-dozen couples attempting a Charleston on the dance floor and found himself focussing instead on the outlines of an unlit kitchen that awaited him across the suburbs. Then, abruptly, they were in the final chorus and Jake yelled back at him to take a solo on the bridge. He could feel the whole eight bars taking shape in his brain, the melodic outline of Max Roach, the space and texture of Tony Williams. With the front line hitting a staccato chord at the start of every second bar, he went into his solo, helplessly feeling the space take up its own predictable, almost military, shape—as if he were somehow moonlighting from the Defence Academy. The crowd seemed to love it though, this balding, bearded, paunchy man rattling dramatically round his kit, though the front line, he knew, could take it or leave it. After a solo like this the final eight always seemed to Roy like some sad hole that only he was peering into—while for everyone else it was the roaring climax of the song. Almost immediately Roy began dismantling his kit and packing the drums away into canvas covers. Earlier there would have been "a drink or three", as Jake used to say, but that feeling in the band had gone now and Roy was happy enough just to be packing up and on his way.

"Great solo, Mr Porter. You play here often?"

Roy looked back up over his shoulder and kept on unscrewing the bass drum pedal. The face was thick-featured, the hair already receding a little.

"You remember me?" The man gave an enigmatic, self-satisfied smile. "2E4? Lyneham High, 1976?"

Roy stood up, the bass drum pedal in his hand.

"Yeah, let me see now. Sat next to Frankie Martino, right?"

"Right!" he said, still smiling. "Benny Elwood." He held a middy in each hand." Drink for old times?"

Roy looked his benefactor straight in the eye. Benny Elwood, the biggest smart-arse in 2E4, now clearly an insurance salesman. "Thanks," said Roy, taking the beer. In his mind he was still unscrewing wing nuts and slackening skins. Surviving these days on light ale mainly, Roy was surprised by the full, yeasty strength of the beer— and by the residue of anger he could still feel even nineteen years later.

"Still teaching?"

Roy nodded.

"Not still at Lyneham?"

"No. Barton now . . . Barton College."

"Just the seniors, eh?" Roy thought he could hear the edge of a sneer and looked for the lean, smart-alecky, occasionally vicious fourteen-year-old he remembered but the man's amnesia was total. His face was all contentment, naivety, goodwill.

"You see Frankie, at all?" Roy asked, recalling the insolent downturn of a mouth.

"No, not for years really." Elwood wiped a line of froth off his lip. "Got on to the hard stuff down in Sydney, they reckon." The insurance man looked briefly out through the glass at the darkness of the lake and the hospital lights on the far side. "You know Frankie used to reckon you were the only teacher he ever had who was worth a pinch of . . ."

"Didn't give that impression," said Roy, seeing a sallow, washed-out face in a corner just waiting its chance. The almost elated goodwill on faces such as Elwood's always made him wonder what had been the point.

"Really used to like History, you know. Not that I remember much of it now of course. Tudors and Stuarts, wasn't it? Henry the Eighth and all that. Not bad, eh?"

"Not bad." Roy fiddled impatiently with the wing nut on the top of his cymbal.

"First time I've heard you play actually. They always reckoned you played around the pubs." Elwood stared for a moment out over the crowd. "Used to play a bit myself years ago. You know, rhythm guitar. Before the wife and kids arrived, that is." Roy nodded, realising the man had probably been drinking beer at this strength all afternoon. Once, with most of them anyway, he would have felt bound to return the shout and talk on for a while, even get slightly sentimental, but now all he wanted to do was load up the old Sigma and get going. "You used to be married yourself, if I remember."

"Yeah," Roy put the glass down near the piano. "Well, good to see you, Benny."

"Yeah," said Elwood, standing there with his empty glass. "See you round maybe."

There was a time when he would have shaken hands but now he simply went straight on unscrewing the big ride cymbal from its stand and, looking up, saw the man drift back to a couple of friends at the bar. The smell of that particular classroom, a close, almost dizzying smell like wet jumpers, rose in his nostrils. He was relieved to see he could still deliberately wipe it away.

For a drummer though it was always like this. By the time the kit was back in the wagon the guys in the band were mostly gone. Sometimes Ken, the clarinetist, gave him a hand but tonight he'd vanished already, gone with his little clarinet case somewhere during the talk with Benny Elwood. In the Sigma now, as he felt for his keys, the drums were big, dark shapes behind him. If he had a smash the bass drum would clock him neatly on the back of the head. It was night completely now, the hospital lights shattering on black water as Roy swung out onto the curves of Alexandrina Drive. The radio had clicked on with the ignition. "And here are the main points again. The Prime Minister says today that he will visit Washington again next month. The death toll from the rail disaster in Uttar Pradesh reaches eighty-two. President Redman denounces Cuba in person at the United Nations in New York . . ."

Roy shoved a cassette in the tapedeck's mouth. It cut in halfway through Elvin Jones's solo on "A Love Supreme", 1964. The cabin seemed to fill with thirty years' thunder, organised but unpredictable, infinitely fluent, seesawing now to a climax as the Sigma felt its way round the lake's edge, its headlights whitening the gums or sweeping out across the water. Then it was on up through Yarralumla, Curtin, Lyons, to a carport rich with cobwebs, and his own cold kitchen.

2

A single spoon, rattled in an empty cup, slowly rolled back the sound of eighty people talking in a room too small for them. "Ladies and gentlemen, could I have your attention a few moments." Roy looked up from his coffee. It was Cy Goodwin in friendly mode. "Firstly a warm welcome back to you all for term two—and I see we have just two new faces this time." He glanced down through half lenses at a note in his hand.

"Firstly, Tom Jeffries. Where's Tom? Ah, yes. Tom is replacing Alan Thompson in the Design and Technology area." A young man already in a grey lab coat stood up and nodded slightly, a faint smile. Roy found he was already unable to recall accurately the quiet, almost transparent man who had just stepped aside. Only ten days ago he'd left the college after a dozen years, taking with him just a few of Cy's easily spun sentences and the standard issue nickel-plated spoon. Roy peered down thoughtfully into his coffee.

"And, let's see now . . . we have Elizabeth Sexton, on the English staff. Libby, isn't it? Stand up, Libby. Take a bow. Libby's replacing Annie Lansdown who's on leave for the rest of the year. Welcome Libby." At the end of the room down near the urn a sandy-haired, broad-featured woman stood up and smiled. Though there was more than a fleck of grey in her hair by now, she reminded Roy of—seemed almost to overlay—a girl he'd taken out at university, an intense, cheery girl with a large dose of social conscience. She had it, Roy discovered, from her father; a professor and a man who had been the first of his teachers to give the impression that the opinion of young Mr Roy Porter might possibly be of some consequence and Roy even now remembered him with a distant gratitude. As other eyes moved away Roy still had his eyes fixed on her, bemused by the similarities, the past overlapping the present.

"I need hardly say," Cy Goodwin went on, "that there may of course be further changes in terms three and four after the mid-year census in June." It was a comment Roy hardly took in. These new rigidities, these countings of souls, had been going on for two years now, ever since the Liberals with their "born again" John Quarry had finally got back in. "First in, last out." That used to be the understanding and even a non-unionist like Cy Goodwin had at least used it as a starting point. But the curves and planes of Libby Sexton's face were a good deal more interesting. There was a humour and flexibility there, he saw. She'd have her opinions clearly but she wasn't a woman to tire you out before you started. His singleness at the end of these seven years was like a possession now, a loved old car you could only think of trading in for something of much greater value.

"Any other announcements?" Cy Goodwin turned to his Admin Level Twos who each obliged with three or four reminders. Confirm class lists as soon as possible. Quotas for photocopying. Computer security. Student fees. Roy heard them all flick past, unoppressed by déjà vu.

"Any other announcements?" Social club, tea and coffee club contributions, projected staff dinner, May 12. Any takers? Roy, who often missed these things, found himself raising a hand. So did Libby Sexton, he noticed. Maybe he'd be playing that night. What was it anyway? A Friday? They could get young Dennis Buckley in that case. He still tended to speed up a little but he'd slow down over time.

"Any further announcements?" No one. The noise swept back like the release of a freeze frame. Roy shouldered his way forward to wash up his mug at the sink. ROY PORTER, it said in white and blue. He'd had to speak firmly to one or two parvenus who didn't, it seemed, read uppercase print. His mug, like his window seat in the staffroom, was something conferred by the years and not to be given up lightly. He hung it on its peg in the bottom left hand corner. On the way out he picked up the day's announcement sheet which, even as he did so, he knew he'd forget to read out to the class. It was like that somehow with Line Six. He often forgot the roll too. It was as if he and they conspired somehow to ignore the administration absolutely.

3

"And what about this one, Roy? Number two. 'World War One started by accident, World War Two by . . .?' "

"Design. Can't you read, you people?" said Roy, ironically. His handwriting was notorious.

"Jeez, Roy. Why don't you use a processor like everyone else?"

"Well, maybe. You never know. One of these days." Actually Roy did have an old Remington at home but these he'd written up by hand the session before. The topics he'd used in earlier years didn't seem relevant any more. He'd rather had in mind to extend number two by adding "How will World Three start?" but decided that could wait till second semester—International Affairs since 1945.

"Okay," Roy said, leaning back in his chair. "Let's run over what we said last term about Versailles." He noticed Tanya at last stop filling in Ann-Marie on the ten days she'd spent down in Sydney with some "neat friends of mum's" and start to look interested. "Who were the Big Four at Versailles?"

"The US."

"Britain."

"France."

"And?"

"Italy," said the normally silent Maria with a slight smile.

"And who didn't get asked?"

"Germany."

"Austria."

"And?"

"Russia."

"What about Ho Chi Minh?" said Hamilton Jack, lifting a casual foot down off the desk at last.

"Or Nguyen Ai Quoc, as he was known in those days," said Roy. "He did get to scamper in the corridors but that's not quite the same thing, I guess." He looked around the room. There were about twelve of them. The computer said twenty but eight were almost always absent. Never the same eight, though a few were fairly chronic. Sometimes it made him feel defensive but you never knew the real reasons. Hamilton Jack, for instance, Roy knew about him—played three nights a week in a rock band but seemed to spend the other four reading history, rather more than Roy himself spent these days. In the first nine weeks on World War One he had never quite made Monday first session or Friday second. Often he missed more but when the essays were due they were always there, and the test results to go with them. Roy himself was almost always on time. There had been a period, seven years back, when things had become confused . . . and Cy had said, rather insufferably, that he knew he (Roy) had "personal problems" but that perhaps he'd better decide which he was going to stick with, teaching or playing. (Funny how you only "played" music.) It was, Cy implied, as simple as that, though he understood the Musicians' Union was, shall we say, a little less successful than the Teachers' Federation in the matter of salaries.

"And what were a couple of main weaknesses of Versailles?" Roy said into the gathered faces. "Some people say it was the single most important cause of World War Two."

No one answered. Hamilton looked as if he could easily do so but was too cool to pick up the easy ones. Angela sat there, biro poised, as if to get the answer down should anyone suggest it. Tanya, with her older smile, turned to Ann-Marie to resume the whispered week in Sydney.

"And what do you think, Tanya? What was the problem in central Europe, for instance?"

Tanya looked up, just slightly embarrassed. Roy noted again how her face stopped just short of being disconcertingly photogenic. There were occasional faces which, to an older man, were virtually intimidating. You hardly had the right to ask them questions.

"You mean all those weak states they made from the old Austro-Hungarian Empire?" she said with the pleased smile of a juggler who has almost, but not quite, missed a ball.

"Right. Can anyone list them, north to south?"

"Poland?" said Ann Marie.

"Czechoslovakia?"

"Hungary."

"Yugoslavia," said Dusanka into the overlapping voices.

"Right . . . right . . . I see all is not lost. The holiday has not caused total amnesia anyway."

Roy looked out the window, distracted by some students digging in the garden plot immediately outside. Their teacher, wearing a wide brimmed Stetson, was directing operations but the logic was not obvious. A few students were pulling out the frosted tomato canes. Others were simply standing about. There were at least a couple of goats in that garden somewhere, buried there

12

by a biology class after dissection. "That corpse in your garden," he thought, "has it begun to sprout?" He remembered one of the English teachers observing such a burial and putting that into the announcement sheet.

"And what," said Roy, "was the problem as far as Germany was concerned? Do I hear the word Diktat anywhere? Article 231 perhaps?"

"The Allied and Associated Governments affirm and Germany accepts the responsibility of Germany and her allies for causing all the loss and damage to which the Allied and Associated Governments and their nationals have been subjected," Hamilton Jack intoned. The others, spread in that U shape which focused on Roy, looked at Hamilton with strictly rationed admiration and a deal of irritation. While they stayed up into the midnight silences finishing their Maths assignments or writing up their Chemistry pracs Hamilton, they knew, was out at Marmaduke's or the Tangarine Palace getting paid. Or else he must be sitting there at home with his feet up reading the whole of the Dewey 900 shelf. He seemed to take the past seriously enough but not the future, or not his own anyway. There was no real money in music, everyone knew that, and that included the string quartets and wind groups that scraped and blew so earnestly up there in the Music department.

"And what did Corporal Hitler, aka Schickelgruber, think of Article 231, Tanya?"

An hour was always just a bit much for Tanya. Between a "neat weekend" in Glebe and the opinions of a mad housepainter already dead for fifty years there could be no real competition.

"I'm not sure," she smiled, "but I reckon he wouldn't have liked it too much."

There was a general movement of books into bags, polite at first; but it was all too clearly time to go.

"Okay, we'll leave it at that," said Roy, gathering his papers. "Make sure you read chapter nine for tomorrow."

Hamilton Jack followed him out the door. "Hey, Roy, did you hear what Redman was saying about Honduras in the paper this morning?"

"No."

"He's really putting it right into Cuba. Real ol' Empire of Evil stuff. Ronnie Reagan was nothing. You have a look." He smiled ironically and went into the hook line of a recent video clip song—"It might look good to you baby, but it don't look good to me." They were at the staffroom door now. Roy noticed Libby Sexton in the light from the window bent over her marking. Hamilton turned and called back over his shoulder. "See you later, man."

4

"You mean you've got him too?" Libby Sexton was saying, her hand wrapped firmly around a glass of house red. "What's he like for you?"

"Oh, not bad. When he turns up, that is. He knows his work though."

"But just a mite pretentious?" Libby reached out, forestalling a nearly empty plate of honey chicken rotating on the lazy Susan. "Probably took my unit just to stir."

"He's not a paid-up feminist, I'll give him that," said Roy, needling her with a smile. "Though the girls don't seem entirely opposed to him I've noticed."

"He doesn't impress my lot. They've cottoned on to him very swiftly. 'Mr Cool' they call him."

Roy sat back a little and looked around the table at the sixteen or so who had put their names down for the staff dinner. They were two-thirds of the way through a cheap banquet where braised, indeterminate dishes descended from the air and circled in front of them. Libby deftly swept up a piece of sweet and sour pork and washed it down with a mouthful of wine. Roy had noticed the way she ate—wholeheartedly but stopping just short of

15

being ill-mannered. She drank the same way too. But it was not entirely unrestrained. In an emergency you could tell she'd probably scrape in just below the .08 limit. He liked that sense of the sixties about her, a sense of not having quite grown up, if growing up had to be equated with mineral water, Swan Light, fat free food, no smoking and infinite good sense.

"Sally told me you're a bit of a musician," said Libby, retrieving his attention with a touch on the forearm.

"Yeah. Drummer actually." Even now he felt the old joke surfacing. Five musicians and a drummer. "Trad jazz. Couple of times a week."

"Yeah? I used to live with a drummer once. Rock drummer. Before I got married." She stared down into the discoloured rice in her bowl. " 'Cadillac'. Yeah, that was their name. Made a record at one stage, probably still got it somewhere. Used to play the pubs. You know, Deakin Inn, the Dickson, that sort of thing. What's the name of your group?"

"Southside City Stompers," said Roy. "Not my idea."

"I never really like trad much—or modern jazz, for that matter. Poofter's music, that's what Billy used to say. Billy was the guy . . ."

"Yeah, well."

"But trad's pretty good to drink to, I'll give it that."

Roy smiled. He'd heard that line too.

"What happened to Billy anyway?"

"I'm not sure, really. He went up to Sydney finally. Dead, probably. Or head of a record company." She laughed and Roy could see her taste for the sheer capriciousness of life.

"You're not still married, are you?" It was a dumb question, he knew. She was here by herself after all—and in the staffroom there'd been none of that "Bill says" or "have to drop Ted off" stuff which stamped the married.

16

"No way. Not for the last five years anyway. The kids are gone now too. One down in Sydney. One in Perth. And a little grandson over there too. How about that?" She looked him straight in the face. The printout was complete; "Now you know." And he knew he should have known all that already. They'd been in the same staffroom five weeks now but there was not as much gossip these days as there'd been once and increasingly in recent years he'd developed a habit of phasing out as though suddenly he'd donned an invisible Walkman which played only the purest white noise.

"And what about you, Roy?" She stared him straight in the eye with a playful seriousness. "No, don't bother. Wife left in '88. One son, grown and down in Sydney. House in Lyons. That's all the grapevine's told me so far."

Not a bad database, Roy thought. It didn't sound too cheerful put like that but he had always liked an ironic tone. He saw her look once around the table: at the other teachers gesturing with hands or chopsticks, also the occasional spouse staring into space. "You like these things?" she said. "Is it always like this at Barton? Where's the rest, for God's sake. The English department's a write-off. Just us — and you're History anyway."

"I wouldn't put it quite as brutally as that, Libby. I'm only fifty-five." He smiled. "What about you anyway? You don't mark essays all the time and there's more to life than feminist fiction, I'm told."

"Don't know about that," she said with mock contientiousness. "Quite a few meetings, I suppose. Women's Group. Peace Group. Environment Centre. A few films. That sort of thing."

Roy watched her as she rattled them off, looking for irony, the self send-up. There was only a trace.

"What peace group?"

"A split from the WILPF. Women's International League for Peace and Freedom. We wanted to let men in too."

"What's it called now?"

"League for Peace." She smiled a little as if to acknowledge its quixotic nature. Roy had been on the peace marches of the mid-eighties though never among the organisers. Walking across Kings Avenue bridge with a few hundred, or even a few thousand of the like-minded had, when you considered the odds, produced as much despair as hope. Even so, there weren't too many students who got through his International Affairs since 1945 without a good sense of the hardware poised on either side, and a clear, if impotent, cynicism about the super-powers.

"What have you been doing lately then? Must've kept yourselves out of the papers."

"Oh, you know, the usual. Telegrams to Redman and Andreyev, Flores in Cuba. Petitions to our very own Mr Quarry suggesting we peep out just a little distance from under the umbrella, see what the weather's like and all that."

"What about demonstrations?"

"Bit early yet. We've only got sixty or so at the moment. We were in the last Palm Sunday march though." Libby smiled and rapped him good-humouredly on the wrist. "You mean you didn't see us?"

"Not on the TV anyway." It was quite a few years now since Roy had bothered to march but he could still remember the opening words on this year's local news: "Organisers today were disappointed . . ." Then there'd been some shots of a few hundred marchers coming down off Kings Avenue bridge surrounded by police. HANDS OFF CUBA. That had been one of the signs. Roy hadn't been there and neither, it seemed, had anyone else much,

18

present company excepted. It must have been her easy certainty, that sense of the sixties well preserved, that drove him on to bait her a little.

"What about the Cubans in Honduras? What does the League say about that?"

"American lies mainly, but we did write to Flores seeking confirmation. Even got an answer, though not from the man himself, of course."

"And what about El Salvador?" said Roy. "The Americans are getting pretty bloody edgy there, I reckon. Sandinistas, Cubans. All that jacking up on foreign debts. Where's it all going to end? says Redman." He went into a redneck drawl. "Goddam Russians'll be in Miami next. Gotta stop 'em somewhere, you know. Monroe Doctrine and all that." Then, switching back, he went on. "You've got to be even handed you know. They're both just as big a bastard."

"Okay, okay," she said, "Maybe you'd like to . . ."

"Hey, Roy!" Fred Sykes, the union man, was yelling as he tipped back on his chair behind his wife, Jeanie, who'd been sitting on Roy's right and earlier on had been interrogating him at length about jazz. His voice had a rowdy, almost resentful edge. "What are you gonna have, the mung bean or the lychees and ice cream? C'mon, you two, a little less of the téte-à-tête, eh? Big decisions, that's what we need here. What'll it be then? The gentleman's waiting. The mung bean or . . ."

5

Roy didn't practise much. The drums were such an awkward instrument really. You packed them into cases, you packed them into your wagon, you lugged them into the club, you set them up, bass drum, tom toms, hi-hat, two ride cymbals, then back into the covers again, out the back door, down the steps, into the car, out of the car, into the house, out of their covers, then set them up again here in the second bedroom. It was easier to leave them stacked in their canvas, piled in a corner, but today, Thursday, on getting home from school he had set them all up and was "having a bash", as he once would have called it. A workout, maybe. Once there'd been a routine, warming up on the old rudiments: mamma dadda, paradiddles, flams. But now he was playing solos just for pure pleasure, starting with a fast 4/4 on the cymbals, the sort of tempo you'd try "The Saints" in at the end of a bad night at the football club, the whole band in a hurry to get the hell out, trying for the speed that Parker or Dizzy would use to frighten tyros off the stage, the sort of tempo which if not practised could paralyse a leg or freeze up a wrist. Roy started as if backing "The Saints" and, a couple of choruses later, segued to "Salt Peanuts", the bass drum dropping bombs now instead of the constant chugging away inseparable from trad, the left hand skating round and under the beat, attacking it from all directions like the short sharp jabs of a bantamweight. Then suddenly he cut the tempo in half, pulling back from the edges of his technique, as if remembering comments overheard: "Roy's chops are pretty basic but his time is okay." He went on more slowly now, abandoning the thirty-two bars with its little bridge and disappearing into pure sound, into the texture of it, the tenor sound of the tom toms, the random bass drum punctuations, the scattered patterns racing on the snare, the brassy overlapping wash of the cymbals, two large rides and a twelve-inch splash. Patterns heard, absorbed from Blakey, Roach or Elvin Jones surfaced, simplified, as if arranged by their own volition in time and space but always falling short of the platonic outlines, the absolute of which any solo of his could only ever be a shimmery imitation. New York, for jazz, would always be the centre and everything else, according to its distance, must be provincial. Was Canberra perhaps the furthest point on earth from the Big Apple? It felt like it sometimes. Often, really. You could hear it in the local rhythm sections, particularly in modern jazz; sturdy, steady, well-intentioned, even swinging in a kind of way (if you cared to stretch the definition). But when the Americans (black or white, it didn't seem to matter) padded out on stage you could tell from the first snap of the snare, from the first plucked A of the bass that it would only be a moment now till lift-off. They had a lightness, a tightness, that fullness of range from the rich wooden depths of the lowest bass notes to the cutting high edge of the smallest cymbal. Roy played on into his dissatisfaction, a cul-de-sac of limitations. He splashed into a final, anarchic round on the cymbals, crashing down on them angrily as the overtones lapped and blurred and grew finally thin like a radio just off the station. Then somewhere he noticed another sound, outside his creation, suspended there just beyond the edge of hearing, the first two notes of a 4/4 pattern, the last two left as rests. It was the telephone. He slipped out from behind the kit and strode towards it down the hall. He picked up the receiver just in time to get the dial tone and reflected how just before you used the phone there was that sense of anticipation and how when you picked it up like this in an empty house it was already only an echo.

6

Well, it hadn't been too bad, Libby Sexton thought as
she stepped out of the shower and into the towel she'd
warmed on the heater. That Roy Porter had certainly
stirred them. "I may be new to this," he'd said, "and maybe
there's not much we can really do but surely we can at
least cut back on the paper and get to the point." "Sorry,"
Lena had said, "but we're on funding at the moment.
Maybe you'd like to raise that under Any Other Business?" Lena, especially when she was in the chair, had
one of those voices that tilted upwards at the end of each
sentence as if it were forever checking its auditor's
comprehension or seeking agreement. Libby found the
same quality in her own voice at times but at least she
was conscious of it. She rubbed the towel around her neck
and shoulders, watching her breasts blurred but abundant
in the steamed-up mirror. The bathmat she stood on was
an island on a sea of rich, red tiles. The unit, she knew,
was a luxury really. It took her right to the edge of her
pay but that didn't worry her now the way it once would
have. Sometimes she felt as if her life had been one long
pilgrimage to this luxury, a really decent en suite
bathroom complete with central heating. As she stood

there she had a sense of her own body as it had been at certain checkpoints in her life: at ten, at twenty, at thirty-five and now at fifty. In a way she was more content with it now than she had been when it had been firmer. There was a fullness there which, generously interpreted, stopped just short of being fat.

She was glad she'd talked him into it now. And smiled a little at his mixed motivations. He'd given the meeting a lift though. The whole group, she knew, were "burnout cases", the older ones who'd started way back in the sixties and even the younger ones who'd surfaced from the eighties. That vigils idea had been a clincher. She was still surprised at how easily it had gone through though he'd never mentioned it to her beforehand. "Even-handedness, that's what you need," Roy had said when the meeting at last had got around to Any Other Business. "One fist each. First the Russians, then the Yanks. There's been enough of bastards like Quarry scoring points with his 'running dogs of Moscow' line. If we get a bomb it'll be made in Smolensk, no doubt, but the button might just as well have been pushed in Washington when you think of why it's on its way." Alternate Sundays, that was the plan and start in with the Russians. Libby had been impressed by his fluency and that bedrock of concern which lay beneath the cynicism and quiet jokes in the staffroom. She'd found herself looking at him sharply— as if, for the first time in weeks now, he'd suddenly come into focus. The details separately were unimpressive: balding, greying with that rough-trimmed beard still flecked with ginger, the small paunch, the forgettable and out-of-fashion polo–neck jumper and cords. Not that she was such a great one for fashion herself. But somehow, when he was on his feet and speaking, the components together were something more than the shopworn sum of his parts.

She stepped into her pyjamas and thought as she did so how in another context she might just as easily be taking them off or letting them be taken off. Ten years ago when AIDS was still a gay disease there would have been no problem. A couple of dinners, a movie or two, would be more than enough preliminaries for two divorcees but even with all the screening, the turnaround tests, the talk of vaccines that never quite came good, it was clear that sex would never really be the same. She walked across the carpet, enjoying its soft pile on the soles of her feet, and climbed up into the big brass bed with its four cupolas, flicked on her bed lamp, flicked off her electric blanket. The days of sex as recreation or memoir of a night's goodwill had gone forever even though, ironically, her risk of conception had vanished with them. It still entertained her a little, however, to imagine the body of Mr Roy Porter under those cords and jumper . . . which parts were hairy, which parts less so, what that paunch would be like rubbing up against her back or climbing over on top of her, the beard rubbing in hard against her neck. She sat up for a moment, remembering to set the radio clock forward fifteen minutes (that photocopying before first session) and inadvertently caught the midnight news.

"And now a news flash from Managua. Reports today have been confirmed that the Honduran government has fallen and President Saliente has been airlifted to the United States. Rebels now control the key points of Tegucigalpa and are dealing with isolated pockets of resistance." Libby turned off the radio and bed lamp; then lay on her back staring at the sudden blackness of the ceiling. As an old Leftist she knew where her sympathies lay. There were too many Somozas, too many Salientes, not to be sure of that, but even so she did think of exactly what those "isolated pockets of

25

resistance" might be; the slumped, collapsing bodies that might be those of death squads and informers and just as well might not. And yet the embarrassment, the chagrin for Redman and all he represented, delivered, even at this distance, more than a little satisfaction.

7

Cy Goodwin motioned him into a chair, an armchair which faced the windows and a rubber plant silhouetted against the venetians. The winter morning came in around it, slatted and sharp. Cy Goodwin had swung around in his chair from reading something and looked down on Roy from an extra foot or so in height. The fact that he was five or so years younger only made it more irritating.

"Just a small one, Roy." For a moment he looked uncertain how to start. "I was talking to a parent the other night, a parent of one of your Line Six students. He seemed a bit . . . how would you say? . . . uneasy? about some of the things going on in your class."

Roy sat forward on the edge of the armchair. "And just what did he reckon was the problem, Cy?"

"He wasn't too specific really. Something about too much discussion, not enough notes."

"Who was it anyway?"

"I'd rather not say at this stage. Suffice to say that he's also a teacher."

"History?"

"No. Maths, actually."

27

"What else did he say?"

"Seemed to think you were giving them too many personal viewpoints. 'Propaganda rather than facts', as he put it."

Roy did a quick roll call in his head, passing over and then coming back to Angela Marsden, Angela with her ready pen and her thirst for information. He'd met the father at the Parent-Teacher night last term and also remembered him from some Federation strike meetings in the early eighties, eloquently outlining the conservative case (the year before he got the principal's job at Hackett College and withdrew from the Federation altogether on a "point of conscience"). The daughter though was harmless enough, never volunteering an answer but always knowing it when pressed. Eighteen out of twenty she'd got in the last term test.

"Well, I do encourage them to have their own view and think about the moral issues involved."

"And your own opinion?" asked Cy, swinging away in his chair with just the beginning of an ironic smile.

"Just one among several," said Roy, "though I suppose it carries a bit more weight." Then he almost laughed. "With the possible exception of our mutual friend, Hamilton Jack." Roy knew that Cy had had some words, some very serious words, with Hamilton about his future and the need for a "balanced package". Cy Goodwin, despite his apparent bonhomie, was capable of a great "seriousness"; insufferably so at times.

"It's not Hamilton we're concerned with in this case, Roy. I can tell you that much."

"Who is it then?" he asked, repressing a smile at the image of Angela he had in his mind even as he spoke.

"I'd rather not say. Perhaps we should just leave it with the recommendation that you give a greater emphasis to the facts and a little less prominence to your own opinion. I think that would satisfy the parent concerned."

"Now hang on, Cy. Maybe I'd better talk to this guy directly. I'm not going to have a half-baked Maths teacher, ex-Maths teacher, telling me how to run my history classes, and through a go-between at that."

"Don't get too excited, Roy," said Cy, swinging away again to look at something on his desk. "He only said it in passing."

For some seconds Roy was left sitting there. He was just about to get up and go when Cy Goodwin swung around on his chair and said: "I've just got the confirmation on the latest transfer policy." He started to read from a letter in his hand. *"In areas which prove to be overstaffed when the new formula is applied, priority in regard to compulsory transfer will be given equally to the needs of the school and to those teachers who have been at a school for seven years or more.* Now that would put some people right in the line of fire, wouldn't it? When was it you came to Barton, Roy? 1980? That's fifteen years for a start. Just have to see how the numbers pan out, eh?"

"You're not trying to tell me something, are you, Cy?" said Roy as Cy swung away again to put the paper back on his desk. Though Roy was used to taking instructions from his chronological juniors there were certainly moments when it became difficult. "Shape up or ship out? That the general drift?"

"I wouldn't put it quite like that, Roy. It's not up to me really. It's purely a matter of student enrolments and a formula. I just make the recommendations. The Chief Education Officer makes the final decision."

"Well, I certainly don't intend to go, Cy. You may as well be clear on that." And he felt himself wanting to add "And I bloody well won't be going either, if it

29

comes to that. It's a damn comfortable little niche and I'm quite happy to see out my time in it." He felt an angry tightness in his throat he'd not felt since Betty left or, before that, since those classes like Benny Elwood's when they really put the pressure on—last period Friday, for instance.

"Well, it's early days yet, Roy, but I thought I might as well put you in the picture."

"Okay ... thanks," said Roy, chewing on the cliches as he picked up the folder and books he'd put down on the coffee table. "Is that the lot now?"

Then, suddenly, Cy seemed more congenial. He had a way of doing that and got up from his chair to see Roy out. "That's all for the moment anyway. As I said it's just a matter of numbers really."

Roy was at the door and on his way when he heard from behind him Cy's valedictory "And how's the music these days?" An answer to which had never been required.

8

"So what was Operation Barbarossa again, Tanya?"
Tanya looked up at him sleepily, as if surfacing from
a great depth. She sometimes used a touch of eyeshadow
which seemed to intensify the effect. Monday mornings
were usually like this. "Barba–rossa. You know, Red
Beard." And he tweaked his own ginger-grey one.

"That was the Nazis going into Russia, right?" said
Tanya, surprising herself.

"And the date?"

"You've got me there."

"June, 1941," said Angela Marsden quietly. Roy
glanced around to his left hardly recognising the voice.

"And why did Hitler set off six weeks late?" He looked
around for Hamilton Jack, for the information, for an
argument, maybe—but Hamilton, it had long been clear,
could not be expected to make a nine o'clock class, let
alone on Monday.

"'Cause the Australians held him up in Greece and
Crete," called Scott, as if to supply Hamilton's missing
sense of irony.

"Right," said Tanya, "That's right. I remember now.
the Aussies and the Kiwis held him up until the Russian

winter got him, and that was the beginning of the end."

"Well something like that has been suggested by some well known historians," said Roy, leaning back in his chair. "Mainly Australians though." He looked across at Angela and remembered the interview with Cy Goodwin. "Wouldn't want to be too dogmatic about that." Despite her father Angela had the kind of purity of expectation that even the most hardened teacher would hesitate to disappoint. It was not just highmindedness or prissiness (the principal of Hackett College had the family allowance of those) but a sheer openness, a clarity of spirit—and of skin, for that matter. "What do you think of that argument, Angela?"

"— "

"You think it was the only factor in Hitler's defeat?" She'd gone quiet again now. "What are some other campaigns we might consider? In '44 say?"

"The D-Day invasion?" she suggested. "June '44." Yes, he could hear Hamilton saying in absentia, but Hitler was already on the run by then. Without the Red Army tying him down it's not very likely the Americans would have got a foot ashore at all.

"That's dead right, Angela, but how important do you think the Russians were overall?"

There was still silence. Roy looked at the faces around the room and then briefly out the window where the fallow earth of the garden plot still had its frosted sharpness. The winter had a long way to go yet.

"What do you think, Scott?"

"Well, I dunno. They were pretty basic, I guess."

"No way the allies would have won without them," said Roy. Was that fact or opinion?

"Well, what about the Russians in Central America now, Roy?" said Tanya. She was fully awake now and delighted sometimes in the ease with which she could lead Roy sideways from a topic.

"Well, I don't know that that's relevant right here, Tanya, but . . ."

"Some people say," said Dusanka, by which Roy knew she meant "my father", "that the Russians are the real force behind all these guerrillas. First the Cubans; then the Sandinistas. Honduras, El Salvador, Costa Rica. It's all the same. It's the Russians everytime. Russian advisers. Russian weapons."

"Well, that is one view, Dusanka. President Redman's anyway. And our own Mr Quarry's, no doubt, but that doesn't mean . . ." He paused, aware of the detour being proposed, and decided to take it anyway. "If you looked at the record of the US in Central America—and we do something on that next term—you'd know that the revolutions in these countries are not just a little dreamchild of the KGB. You do know about the death squads and so on?"

Actually he knew that in the case of Costa Rica the argument was a good deal less true. The president beleaguered there was not, at this stage anyway, the simple Somoza or Batista figure whom the Left loved to hate. For Central America anyway, Costa Rica seemed almost to approach democracy and give some credence to Redman's rhetoric. Its decision not to maintain an army was unparallelled in Latin America and, as far as he knew, in the world. It did, however, have a remarkably large police force.

"Well, what do you think should be done?" he heard a voice, female, ask to his left. It must have been the first question of this kind Angela had ever asked. Normally it was "Could you repeat the date, please?" or "How do you spell . . .?" Roy, remembering the interview with Cy, was wary for a moment. Fact or opinion? But the expression on her face was as guileless, as pure, as ever.

"You mean Redman—or us individually?"

"Either, I suppose."

"No telling what Redman might do. He would have sent in the marines long ago if that were still an option. I don't think congress is too keen on that. Yet, anyway." He could almost hear Hamilton Jack say it so he said it himself anyway. "Of course, he could have another shot at the Bay of Pigs and get it right this time." The Bay of Pigs was not due till the end of next term but Roy suddenly remembered, as he'd done more than once these past few weeks, how at twenty-two he'd been listening to the static of an old valve radio at university as the Russian ships bore down on the Kennedy blockade. For him, that October was in some ways closer than next term. For them it was just another minor item in the millennia that stretched away backwards from '78, the year of their hatching on the planet.

"Bay of what?" said Angela.

"Don't worry," said Roy, hearing the movement in the corridor from change of class. "We'll do it next term."

9

"See you later then, okay? About seven? You got the address?"

Libby looked up from her desk across the room to where Roy stood framed in the doorway, now almost gone but still leaning back around the corner. Maybe he wanted three separate answers to his three separate questions but she just smiled and reached for her file of essays, "800 words approx" in each. To mark the whole class was, collectively, half a novella or a story by Henry James. They nearly all used processors these days but for some it was just a whole new field for solecisms. A few years ago when she'd been at Weston College for a term it had seemed as if the processor itself could be programmed to print off answers to " *'Madame Bovary, c'est moi.'* Discuss", but even in this old, almost arthritic, convention of the formal essay the student's own personality could sometimes sneak through. She shuffled them a little and flipped through the first four or five. Jane Bowman. That might be a good one. Libby thought briefly of Jane Bowman's pert, confident face. It seemed almost to be photocopied on to the title page as a kind of ground for:

STUDENT Jane Bowman
TEACHER Libby Sexton
UNIT Twentieth Century Fiction: A Retrospective
TOPIC Which novel from your reading of twentieth century fiction is most likely to survive the twenty-first century? In your answer you should also refer to at least three other novels.
WORDS 861
DUE DATE May 26, 1995

Libby adjusted the old one-bar heater near her feet and started to think. An hour on this; then home for a shower. And then the drive to Lyons. She could see herself already looking at the map under the dull inside light of her car, twenty minutes late and having thought she knew where Boondarra Street was. If you'd been in a suburb once you tended to think you knew it but in Canberra, with all its convolutions, this was hardly ever a reliable assumption.

"Bachelor stew and a bottle of red. How about it?" And then after he'd got her agreement, "Why don't you come across about seven then?" That was the way he'd put it, coming up to her at the end of the recess announcements. The sky was dark now and coming down behind her. She could feel it without looking, that windy, early evening darkness down from the snow somewhere. She wondered if Roy had an open fire. She still loved the smell of woodsmoke. The absence of an open fire from her unit in the tower was its only real defect. Two new mortgages, as she and Ned had been only too aware when they settled their house, instead of the one that was almost paid; and just for the pleasure of living alone. Though Ned, she'd rightly suspected, wouldn't be alone for long.

It was strange (or was it so strange?) the way Roy

kept to himself so much in a room of nine younger women—though some, she could see, were not very much behind him in the race to retirement. The whole service was getting to be quite geriatric, everyone knew that. Roy, it appeared, had acquired his desk near the window not long after his arrival in 1980 but at the same time seemed to have found an inward corner and not looked out since. The women were all English teachers and he was "History" but that was only part of it. The endless discussion of moderation methods and students being advantaged or disadvantaged rattled around the room and left Roy pretty much undisturbed. The exchange of recipes and weekend anecdotes, the sighs about their teenage children, went on well enough without his intervention. Even so, and even though Libby had only come to Barton this term, Roy was already, with his ginger-grey, unruly hair, and the broad curve of his shoulders, an essential part of her daily background. She looked across at his desk, almost surprised to find it unoccupied.

"Why don't you come across?" The phrase came back to her now. He'd caught her near the rack where the mugs were hung. She remembered the way she'd smiled, almost flinched, at the unintended double entendre, that compound verb with its transactional nature, the verb "to come across". It took her further back with men than she wanted to go. Those sad boyish necessities, the way they had to prove themselves, the boredom and restlessness afterwards. They'd talked quite a bit now, she and Roy, in certain free times when they seemed almost to have the staffroom to themselves. What about? Well, Cuba, Central America, the economic background there, that Redman speech . . .

Whereas Sons and Lovers *is regarded by many critics as a deeper examination of human psychology it seems*

37

likely that the formal perfection of The Great Gatsby *will . . .*

And other things too. High schools and colleges—the ease of the latter, the impossibility of the former. It was strange to see the way Roy had gone on at times about the high schools. Maybe it was that transfer policy which hadn't quite come off in the late eighties when college teachers were required to spend one year in seven in a high school. She remembered having seen a couple of them who had actually been sent looking lost and nostalgic but Roy seemed to have slipped that net anyway. She knew he was right about them but it was curious, even so, to see the strange filtering effect that fifteen years had had on his memory, making them at once a little better and in many ways worse than they really were. Being less than one term removed from a high school herself she could still hear clearly the noise in the corridors at change of class, the sense of cattle yards, the milling playground, the caustic screech of a thirteen-year-old tart, the sneering silence of a boy kept back at recess. "Put 'em all out to pasture for a couple of years," had been Roy's solution. "That's what Mao used to do and he wasn't all wrong either." You wouldn't catch him going back.

Modernist experimenters like the James Joyce of Finnegan's Wake *and the French writers of the now passe* nouvelle roman (*Nathalie Sarraute, for instance*) *proved in the longer term to be no more than a minor, if necessary, reconnaissance party compared to the broad, forward progress of what the early and seminal, if somewhat chauvinistic, critic F.R. Leavis, referred to as "The Great Tradition".*

Where did she get all that from? Libby wondered. By week five she wasn't much past learning their names. Maybe young Jane had recently acquired a pretentious

friend or two. Or was it a parent she'd had all along—
or a recently obtained one for that matter? She looked
up at the clock. 5:15. And bent down under her desk
to switch off the radiator. Then, standing at the door
for a moment, she looked back over the staffroom, at
the desks spread awkwardly around the walls and piled
high with paper. She wondered suddenly whether the
appearance of such rooms had changed any more than
"the modern novel" had across the whole century. The
fluorescent tubes sent down their clean but sickly glare.
With a flick of the switch she swept it all into darkness
and headed off down the passage to let herself into the
wind.

10

Port in one hand, coffee in front of them, they sat at Roy's fire, staring into the coals. He'd just rerun the interview with young Cy Goodwin, BA, M.Ed., Principal of Barton College. Libby was still smiling at the catch line "How's the music these days?"

"And how is it going anyway?" she said, staring more deeply into the fire. He watched her profile flickering in the light and the edge of her lightly freckled smile. From the side her face had a slight flatness about it; from the front it was an honest kind of breadth.

"Oh, much the same, you know. Thursday nights, Sunday afternoons. But that's not the point, Libby. The point is that I don't want to go and I'm bloody well not going to let Cy push me out either. He's a parvenu, anyway, if it comes to that. Only came in '85—and on a transfer from the office. There used to be a time when it was 'first in, last out' but the union seems to have let that one slide."

"Maybe he'll drop Annie Landsdown while she's away," said Libby. "In that case it'd be me." She poured herself another demitasse of Roy's strong, grainy coffee. It stood, the plunger half down, on a well ringed blackwood table straight from the Danish sixties. Something Betty hadn't wanted maybe?

"No, it's the History not the English where the numbers are down. We spread our offerings right across seven lines and only pick up a few on each. Besides, Cy's more than a bit sick of Roydon Porter right now, I suspect, with that fellow principal chewing his ear and all that."

"Marsden?"

"Yeah, Angela's dad. David Marsden." His voice became mockingly pompous. "Distantly related to the famous Samuel, I believe. Principal of Hackett College. Ex-federationist extraordinaire."

"Well, what about the union, Roy? Have you talked to Fred Sykes yet? He's meant to be pretty strong on things like this."

"Used to be. Selective sellouts, that's the name of the game these days." Roy was on his feet now and walking about. "Takes you back, doesn't it? Remember the halcyon years of Hawke and Fraser when they only cut back by one or two per cent. Now they just key in a new formula and, hey presto, you're 'surplus to requirements'. I think that's the phrase. Especially if they don't like you to start with."

"You may as well talk to him though," said Libby with mild impatience. "Can't do any harm."

"Yeah . . . but still it's only early days yet. Old Cy hasn't said anything concrete yet and the census isn't even due till the end of next month . . ." He tapered off and wandered over to the record player. Underneath it, in open shelves, were about three metres of LPs. He took one which had been lying flat across the top and as he dusted it clean and put it on the turntable he said back over his shoulder, "See what you think of this. Better than talking about old Cy, that's for sure." Probably think it's some Fireside Five routine, Roy thought, and smiled.

41

There was a moment of preliminary, indecisive crackle; then the strident declarations of Bobby Timmons' "Moanin'", piano, bass, drums, trumpet and tenor sax, the definitive hard bop combination, the tonality black as Art Blakey's face on the record cover which he took across to her. "Just listen to the first eight bars of the trumpet solo." And once again, Lee Morgan, trumpeter, came spiralling out from a corner with his sharp elliptical phrases, so unpredictable and yet, in retrospect, so exactly right; Lee Morgan, cut down by his girlfriend outside a New York club twenty-five years ago now but still here on vinyl with all his sassiness. Watching Libby's profile in the firelight, Roy went back another twelve years beyond that to 1958, to sharing such music, or something milder (MJQ, Brubeck, Oscar Peterson) with his first university girlfriend, lying dishevelled but still dressed on a college bed, two heads on the same pillow and staring at the ceiling. He actually listening, hearing the bars flick by, she (who knows?) wondering what he might try next or why he'd not tried it already, testing him out perhaps in a mortgaged house as father of two, thinking of that essay due for Friday, maybe even listening to the music. "Safe sex" of the fifties. Roy allowed himself a smile at the cycles of history.

He moved back to his chair in front of the fire, sweetened his lips on his glass of port and looked at her, still staring into the fire. "Did you think it'd all be funny hats, eh?" She smiled and said nothing. Art Blakey's snapping afterbeat was coming down hard now behind the locked chords of Bobby Timmons running and jabbing along the whole length of the piano. Timmons was another of those early deaths. It was loud, too loud to talk over, too loud to set a mood to lead on to something else. He remembered the Johnny Mathis and Frank Sinatra records that his friends had recommended for

42

such a purpose thirty-five years ago or the Tchaikovsky Piano Concerto No. 2 which was held to be even more effective—that whiff of the sublime.

"What do you really like about it, Roy?" She turned towards him and put down her glass. "It's not that I don't like it. I like all sorts of music but . . ."

"Well, just about everything, I guess." Actually there was something sublime about jazz too, or could be. Coltrane in the early sixties, for instance. It was not the same sublimity that came with the Tchaikovsky strings in all their celestial layers but a sense of four men playing right on the very edge of the planet and not just between the soundproofed walls of a New York studio. It was as if the notes went straight off into space, abandoning the chords, abandoning the scales, abandoning gravity itself and heading outwards, another part of the expanding universe. But you could hardly get words around that.

"The rhythm's one thing, of course. The old 4/4, that continuity, the tension and release. The blowing, too. You know, the improvisation. That above all, probably. The sense that it's not some standard interpretation of some standard piece. Anything can happen. You have to think on your feet, as it were." He looked at her, asking her to overlook his seriousness. "Or on your bum, in the case of drummers." Libby smiled and picked up her glass, spilling it slightly and adding another small stain to the wooden surface.

"What about in the band? The Southside City Stompers?"

"Same thing really. Not as good in some ways, obviously. But better in others." Often, to play the simplicities required of a drummer in the Stompers was just as satisfying as listening to the technique of an Elvin Jones on a good sound system. The gap in quality was acute but to be actually doing it was a powerful compensation. He started to feel self-conscious, as if he were imposing something on her.

"What about you, Libby? Would you rather put on some Rachmaninoff or something? Some folk, maybe . . . You go back that far?"

Libby smiled and put down her glass. She could have been just faintly bored. "Well, I used to like folk. You know, Joan Baez, Bob Dylan in the old days. A bit of Redgum and Eric Bogle in the seventies. Tracey Chapman, maybe. Midnight Oil. I don't go much for the fin-de-siècle plastic you hear these days."

Roy knew that "Just about everything" in most cases meant "Nothing very much" but he didn't hold it against her in the way that he might once have done. Being fifty plus had its advantages. Tolerance could well be one of them. He remembered the dogmatism with which he used to argue with rock'n'roll fans in the early sixties. "It's okay for drinking and dancing maybe but for serious musical nutriment . . .?" Actually that described trad pretty well too but trad was not the music he had in mind even back then, despite his playing it already in pubs on Saturday afternoons for not much more than jugs of beer. He could certainly agree with her about the contemporary pop anyway.

Then, as he looked across at her, he had a sense of how he ought to be hurrying things along perhaps but felt almost too relaxed to do so. The alcohol had had an effect but not the one it would have had a decade or more ago before this new age of caution. You never really knew who was just filling in time waiting for symptoms. It was more pleasant just to sit and listen. Those other complexities could look after themselves. To judge from Libby's closed and possibly attentive eyes that might, or might not, be what she was doing, just sitting and listening. Did it matter really ? Behind him there in 1965 Lee Morgan was dancing and weaving his way through the bridge of "Along Comes Betty", the Benny Golson tune, and soon now Golson himself would be moving in on tenor, reshaping his own melody as though the improvements, the permutations, were endless and all might yet be right with the world.

11

"You finished that essay yet, Hamilton?" Tanya looked out across the quadrangle filled with watery light.

"Well, I've done a certain amount of reading, if that's what you mean."

"You always get good marks though."

"Only place I do," said Hamilton. "You reckon Roy gives me a few extra just for playing the drums?"

Tanya turned and looked him in the face. "You never know, do you. That could explain quite a lot when you think about it."

Hamilton seemed not to know if she was serious or not. "Come off it, Tanya. I'm a rocker, don't forget. That's a pretty low form of life for an old trad muso."

"Same instrument though."

"Only just," said Hamilton, looking out across the cement to where a skateboarder was attempting a small gutter. "You ever heard any trad, Tanya? My dad actually likes it. The names are great, I'll give 'em that. Fats, Jelly Roll, Willie the Lion, Cow Cow—now that's a beauty."

"Cow Cow?" Tanya smiled in disbelief.

"Cow Cow Davenport. You haven't heard of him?"

"What did he play? The milking machine?"

"Piano, I think. Blues piano."

There was a pause. Tanya looked at his legs in those long black jeans which stretched to the opposite bench. "Did you ever hear Roy play?"

"Two or three times, maybe. Once a couple of years back. Over at the Yacht Club. Southside City Stompers they call 'em." He grinned and made a chinging sound with his tongue and teeth, a hi-hat cymbal playing trad. "Keeps good time. No doubt about that."

"Don't tell me they actually let you in?"

"Only a couple of years short of the mark." He gave her a light dig in the ribs. "You reckon I'm a bit youthful, eh?"

"Oh, I wouldn't say that, Hamilton. They all reckon you're a pretty old hand . . . bit of a bastard really." Suddenly she looked serious. "I think someone tried to tell me that actually."

"They did, eh? And who was that?"

"Oh, I don't know." She smiled again. "One of your friends maybe . . . Angela?"

"Angela! Don't give me the . . ." He paused. "You ever meet her dad?"

"No, but I can probably imagine."

"No, Tanya, you can't." He pulled his legs down off the opposite bench and turned towards her. "You should meet him. He's the boss over at Hackett. My Mum knows him. A severe pain in the rear end!" He pulled his knees up against his chest. "You know he complained to the boss here about Roy, don't you? About bias or something! That's a beauty. Roy 'on-the-other-hand' Porter?"

"You mean Angela just . . . dobbed him in?"

"She must have said something. Wouldn't take much to set a nut like Marsden off though."

"So what happened to Roy?"

47

"Rap on the knuckles, slap on the wrist. Something like that. Though I reckon Cy's really got it in for Roy when you think about it. If he's looking around for a transferee . . ."

"Transferee?" said Tanya. "You mean they'd just pack him off like that?"

"Well they might give him one of those silver-plated teaspoons but that'd be about it."

"That's a bit pathetic." She looked across towards the covered way, as if any moment Roy himself might emerge and make a diagonal for the canteen. "Where'd we be without Roy?"

"Could do a lot worse. Old Bozo Tanner, for instance."

"Yeah, but that's not the point," she said. "He's a good teacher. Bit late on the essays maybe—but he knows what he's talking about."

Hamilton glanced across at one of the pine trees where a magpie had just alighted on the topmost limb. "Actually he has got a few gaps if you go looking for them but he knows the right questions anyway . . ."

Tanya groaned with friendly impatience. "You know, Hamilton, sometimes you're nearly as much of a pain as that Angela." She pulled a phrase down out of the air. "Britannica Jack, the walking encyclopedia!"

"Well, if you do a bit of reading, Tanya, you're bound to find something out over time."

"Like the day you get a decent grade in something other than History?"

"Ouch," he smiled. "*Mea culpa*, as Roy would say." He unfolded his legs as if getting up to leave. "Listen," he said, "you want to come down to Kingston after last session? Be a few others there probably. Quick drink or two. All work and no play . . ."

"You should talk."

"Well, how about it?"

"Sorry. Not this time, Hamilton. I've got to work."

"What? On your essay? That's not till . . ."

"No, real work. Shoprite at Deakin on the checkout. Thursday, Friday after school."

"Yeah?" He looked as if he had trouble processing such information. "Checkout chick, eh?"

"You better believe it."

"I do, I do."

"Why not for dinner sometime," she said, looking away. "That might be nice."

"Yeah, well, why not? I'll check in my diary and get back to you!"

She smiled. "Diary now, eh? Getting yourself organised at last?" Then, suddenly, the movement in the quadrangle seemed to intensify. "Speaking of which, don't you have Maths on line five now?"

"Ah no!" said Hamilton, looking disconcerted for the first time. "That Kessler woman threatened to delete me if I didn't show up every session this week. I'll have to get back to you on . . ."

"See you later, Einstein!"

12

Sunday, June 11, 10 p.m. was not a good time to be outside the Russian embassy. They stood, about fifty of them, on the median strip of Canberra Avenue which was as close as the police, who virtually outnumbered them, were prepared to let them go. It had been a day of dirty cloud and wind sweeping down from the Brindabellas and the main range beyond that. They had started the vigil at seven that morning and at various times of the day had numbered up to three hundred or so. These included a politician who addressed them through a loudhailer so weak that whole sentences were swept away by the semis as they trundled down to the Manuka lights. Roy had been there from the beginning—with just a few strategic retreats to the Hotel Kingston immediately behind them. But at ten in the evening they stood around a couple of fire-filled ten-gallon drums, scarves wrapped tight around their necks, balaclavas reducing faces to sets of eyes only. Even the bloody weather's Russian, Roy thought, imagining a comparable group of peasants stooging about outside the Winter Palace in 1905. Well not quite comparable but still . . .

"Bit like something out of Dostoyevsky," he said through his balaclava.

"What's that?" said Libby as another semi rolled past, changing down.

"I said it's a bit like Dostoyevsky or something. You know, standing around in the square hoping to nobble the Tsar with a petition."

"Yeah, right. Though I guess they're not all in the secret police," Libby said, indicating the Federal Police who held the line across the street, the fluorescent lights dusting their shoulders but leaving obscure what Libby supposed to be their fresh and well intentioned faces.

Suddenly about two metres away a car in the right-hand lane slowed down. A window wound down and an indeterminate face spat out. "Why don't you bloody fascists go home?" Libby, whose career in demonstrations went back, off and on, to the mid sixties, had often been called a "commie" but this at least was something new. She glanced over her shoulder at the banner behind her—LEAGUE FOR PEACE—and at another more makeshift placard declaring

WE DON'T WANT TO GO
WASHINGTON, MOSCOW.

"Must've been stirring those Latvians," said Roy, remembering how as darkness arrived a few cars had swung up on the median strip disgorging about twenty men and women in their fifties and sixties. For a time they had shouted in unison "Russia out of Baltic now" but for the last couple of hours, like everyone else, they had simply been huddling from the wind. Roy wondered at the dogged but leisurely look on their faces. They had been at this for decades already and there might well be decades left to go but that didn't seem to alter the imperatives which brought them out here on such

51

a night. A December evening in Riga would be no warmer, Roy supposed.

"Yeah," said Libby. "They're confusing things a bit but you can't stop 'em, or at least not yet." She stared again at the police across the street. "Though I suppose Quarry'll get around to that too in the end. Or maybe the anti-communists will get a kind of papal dispensation." Roy smiled at the almost leathery cynicism in Libby's face and understood a little more about why he was standing here at ten on a Sunday night instead of being in front of his fire in Lyons with some hard bop on the turntable. Though, of course, it *was* his idea, given that it had been Libby who had persuaded him to go to the meeting in the first place. He re-ran the pure logic of his argument at that meeting and wondered how he could have excluded the weather. Perhaps he should have been an economist, not a History teacher.

"Cold enough for you, Roy?" said Libby, as if she were sharing his head. "It was your idea, you know. What do you reckon now? Make any difference one way or the other?" She looked across at the barred and unlit windows of the embassy behind its two metre high fence and its second growth of grevillea. She remembered how some demonstrators had managed to burn it at some stage back in the seventies. "Nice to be on the KGB files as well as ASIO and the CIA."

"Yeah," said Roy with a despondent smile. "It's the least we can do—and the most, too, probably." It certainly seemed to be more than most Canberrans wanted to do on a cold Sunday night, though something slightly more had been attempted two hours back when Roy and Libby had noticed one of their fellow demonstrators scratching an extra message on the back of his placard.

"There," he'd said. "That should liven things up just a little. Used to work quite well against those South

African bastards." He lifted up the sign which was lit by streetlights across the road. TOOT FOR PEACE.

"Well, they can't do much less than that," said Libby to Roy, her mouth an ironic crease. "Doesn't take much to blow your horn." Roy had imagined that there would be a toot here and there, if only as a kind of sardonic counterpoint, but the cars and semis had kept on grinding past and two hours now had gone by without any other sound.

Clearly, Roy realised, it would take more than this ruckus in Central America, these riots and reneging on foreign debts to ruffle the equanimity of this city on wheels which rode so sedately past them down to the lights. A little of their armour-plated serenity had come even to Roy himself back at seven-thirty when a few bars of evensong had blown down from St Paul's on the corner. It had taken him back to those Sunday evenings in his teens, to evensong with his parents, to that collective sense of "let-us-give-thanks-to-the-God-who-guards-our-church-and-may-the-world-take-care-of-itself". Was there some device built into Mitsubishi sedans, Volvo wagons and Mack trucks which produced automatically its secular equivalent? Maybe there was some kind of glass cupola over the whole city. Maybe they all lived in some invisibly sealed diorama. But, if that were so, where was this cold wind coming from? How come it was getting in under the edges?

13

"You're gonna have to give me time on this one Roy," Fred Sykes was saying. "It's not like it used to be, you know." They were standing outside the main block after recess on a clear winter morning. Fred seemed to stare through the bare poplars and into the traffic which ground impartially towards Civic.

"I'm not going. It's as simple as that, Fred. Union or no union." Fred looked him briefly straight in the eye as if to check the resistance there. Roy felt the measuring almost physically on his face and knew that Fred Sykes had nothing much to thank him for really. No more than anyone else anyway. Roy remembered all the times his hand had gone up to oppose those motions Fred put forward when briefly stepping aside from the chair. He remembered times when they'd both just come to the college, when a chance for a fight with Cy or his predecessor would never have been passed up. Not by Fred, anyway. There'd be a deputation at the principal's door almost before he'd finished his pronouncement. There had been times when you'd think twice about Fred's help; it might be more than you really needed.

"Not quite as simple as that, mate. The census'll say

we're one teacher surplus to formula. Someone's got to go." Fred twisted his canvas shoe against the cement as if a candidate might somehow be found there. "Needs of the school and time in the job, they're the two criteria. The federation's never fought either of them really. Not in recent years anyway!"

Roy looked away through the pale bare trunks and felt the sun soak through him right down to the bones in his toes. It didn't stop the sourness rising from his stomach.

" 'First in, last out,' that's the way it used to be."

"Yeah," said Fred, "but only on a system basis now. Tenure in the service, not in the school. You remember that don't you, '91 wasn't it?"

Roy did remember it actually, the mass meeting after school on the issue, with just two hundred of three thousand turning up. Roy, already nine years at Barton and enjoying it, had been one of them. He remembered the tone but not the words of the motion. Something about "the union demands" and the "educational benefits of security of tenure". Had Fred been there or not? He couldn't remember now. But he remembered other meetings a decade before that when Fred and a pack of three or four others were forever moving the "overthrow of the Fraser government and the return of a Labor government sworn to socialist principles." Probably Fred wasn't there, not in '91 anyway. For people like Fred tenure at a school was obviously a bourgeois and divisive issue, even if it did give the principal a certain power he wouldn't have had otherwise. All government schools were equally good—so why did it matter where one worked? Then with the Liberals back in there'd been the "mid-year rationalisations" and this "early retirement" business.

"Don't know what you're worried about," Fred went on. "He didn't mention a particular school, did he?"

"No, too early yet but he made it very clear that I'd be the one to go."

Fred glanced at his watch and backed off slightly towards the door. "Yeah, well, as I said . . ."

"You are going to call a meeting on it at least?"

"Well, that depends."

"On what?"

"I better give O'Connell a ring first. See what they're doing at other schools. This mid-year census . . ."

"It'd carry a bloody sight more weight if we had a motion through here, wouldn't it?"

"Well, maybe," said Fred. "But you'd have to get it through first. It's not really the sort of thing people are prepared to go out on these days. Not under this government, anyway, with all this 'management-initiated retirement' about." He looked at Roy with what could have been either disdain or sympathy. Fred Sykes was some five years younger. Roy remembered having seen his birthdate on a form at one stage. 1945. "And that could be a bit of a problem in your case, mate, if we push it too hard." Fred glanced again at his watch. "Got to go now anyway. Line Four Economics." Fred was already halfway to the door. "I'll give O'Connell a ring and let you know tomorrow. Okay?"

Roy kept staring at the trees and felt rather than saw Sykes slip away sideways through the main door of the college. There was a chipped garden bench beside the entrance and Roy who normally would have headed off for the staffroom sat down for a moment and stared dully at the traffic flickering through the trees. Between a couple of silver birches he noticed the back of the college sign. Fifteen years he'd been passing that sign, swinging past it at 8:55, absorbing subconsciously its curious typography—a style which had once had a two year vogue and now had disappeared. Fifteen years. He felt a strange thrust of rejection, not unlike that which he'd experienced once in his earliest days on drums when the band had disintegrated only to reform a few weeks later with a new drummer. Barton had been a comfortable kind of identification, "What do you do? Teach? Really? Whereabouts? . . . Barton College? Yeah, what's it like?" "Great actually." And then depending on mood and, in the old days, on alcohol intake, he'd go on to list selected virtues. Now it seemed young Cy had got to him at last. Never did trust that bastard, he thought . . . and as for Fred Sykes. You'd swear that Cy had made the bastard an offer he couldn't refuse. Hard to see what. Though, of course, Sykes himself had come to Barton only two years later than Roy and there was that other criterion. Maybe next time, it'd be Social Science. "You never know, do you, Fred?" Roy could imagine that conversation very well in the same sun-slatted office.

Even in the late eighties with these sorts of cutbacks, transferring Fred would have been unthinkable. Now, with Quarry in power and local government come at last, it was just a matter of the union collecting its dues and keeping its collective head down. Roy remembered as he sat there the first strike he was ever on back in '68 with the NSW outfit and old Jack Whalan. There was a nice sense of solidarity and peril. No one quite knew where this could all lead. It was the first time teachers had ever struck and now he could hardly even remember the issues—salaries probably, class sizes, maybe?—but he did recall the altruistic tone . . . "In future years the members of this Federation will look back and say this was the year of the sixty-eighters." It had sounded a bit too fruity at the time but now, at this seemingly immeasurable distance and especially in his situation, sitting and staring blankly into the traffic, Roy heard a poignant, even a noble ring to it. That sense of the old Albert Hall filled shoulder to shoulder with solidarity had gone, he couldn't quite say when. Just worn away perhaps. There was none of it now. The Sunday vigils outside the embassies had a little of the same edge but there was a despondency about them, "the least we could do," as Roy himself had put it that night in the committee meeting. The least Sykes could do was hold a protest meeting, even if only for old times' sake. He'd have a yarn with Libby for a start. She was a damn sight better value than anyone else around here, that was for sure.

14

Roy, just on five minutes late, steered his way with some relief into the library armed with the standard black coffee and two Nice biscuits he'd collected on his way in from the foyer. It had been so cold outside, a strong dark wind that had almost blown him across the carpark. Most of the English and History teachers were already seated at tables with parents, nodding their heads in sympathetic discourse. Libby, it seemed, was a little late also to judge from a quick scan of the reading room, though she could possibly be in that other area around the corner there behind the stacks. He smiled at Sally Cowan who didn't have any business yet and rounded the corner of the Dewey 900 stack. Libby wasn't there either. He sat down at an empty table and took a crunch on one of the Nice biscuits. It was all so predictable, the biscuit and the whole evening. How many of these things had he been to now? Say three a year for thirty-three years — ninety-nine? Why did it always have to be the parents of the conscientious showing how their kids got to be that way? How did one go on with these little litanies of self-congratulation? "Yes, David just needs to refine his essay technique a little and he'll be operating at second year university standard already." Or the occasional "Could contribute a little more to class" for the bright but silent ones—the Angela Marsdens, for instance. Though Roy certainly had no desire to encounter "the Rev." David Marsden, as it were, principal of Hackett College—who, right now, was probably introducing a visiting luminary at an Ed Admin meeting across town somewhere.

Roy was already so bored he was tempted to dunk his second biscuit in his coffee just by way of variation. Tonight, he suspected, would be one of those affairs where you spent half the time flipping through a couple of books and waiting for the two or three parents who could be bothered checking you out. He was beside the 900s anyway, a favourite spot; it offered an opportunity to catch up on his reading a little. Roy rather regretted that his reading had somehow lost its momentum in the last few years. In the early days and even when he'd first come to Barton he would read right around a topic, attempting a total immersion. At some stage, however, in the last ten years he had slipped back into a kind of perfunctory revision, a keeping-up by skimming again the basic texts to bring things back into focus. Now it was possible for a student like Hamilton Jack to be reading and quoting a book Roy had never heard of. But he still had the structure there, the framework of the building, which was always the basis anyway and beyond which not too many students at this level could really be expected to progress. If they got the outlines right and some of the main issues they'd be doing well enough and those at least were something Roy Porter could still provide.

He took a sip at the hard black coffee and over the rim of his cup he could see a lean man in a business suit striding between the tables towards him. Roy got up to shake his hand. There was no doubt the man knew whom he was looking for.

"Mr Porter?"

"Roy."

"Stuart Jack. Hamilton's father." The man paused and gave Roy an appraising look. "He gave me a pretty good description."

"Not too good, I hope," said Roy.

The other man smiled and went on. "Seems to be doing well enough at History anyway. Always his favourite actually, even back in high school. You seem to have him working well."

"Yeah," said Roy. "He's one in a hundred, Hamilton. He really reads for a start. There's no substitute for that."

"Yes," said Stuart Jack. "That and these rock bands are about all that he runs to these days." He paused for a moment. "And girls, maybe. Or is that implied when you say rock bands?"

Roy liked the man's irony and wondered what line he was in. Public service probably. That always gave one a nice sense of irony. Senior Executive Service. Level Two. That would be about it. You got to know these levels even when you weren't a part of it. Probably did a fair bit of working back. He pretty clearly hadn't been home from the office yet.

"How's he been in class?"

"Invaluable," said Roy. "When he's there."

"Still cutting the odd one, eh? That figures. He's been a bit spoiled, I'd have to admit that. His mother . . ."

"Doesn't affect his scores though," said Roy. "Probably does us all good to be reminded we're not completely indispensable."

"I don't know, Roy," he said, dropping into the informal mode he'd probably resort to at important points in inter-departmental meetings. "He's been damn lucky with his teachers, overall. All the way through, really. Had a very good one back in Year Eight. She really got him started."

61

"But not such a good one in Maths, eh?"

"Well," said Stuart Jack, "I'm not sure that's the only factor but . . ." He sat back a little, easing his long legs under the table. "That's really why I dropped in tonight, to have a yarn with the current victim. She does seem a little less than impressed."

"Less than impressed?" said Roy with slight smile.

Stuart Jack smiled too. "Maybe she just hasn't heard him on the drums yet."

Roy nodded absently, "No. Probably not." He was watching what looked to be a forty-five year old version of Tanya walk towards him across the room and stand at a polite distance, waiting. Stuart Jack, seeing the lapse in Roy's attention, looked back over his shoulder.

"Yeah, well, thanks, Roy. Good to meet you." He pushed back his chair over the carpet, stood up and reached out to shake Roy's hand.

"Yeah, okay," said Roy and was already waving Tanya's mother into the just vacated chair.

"You don't have to tell me who *you* are," he smiled.

"Gina Volska," she said, leaning in and shaking his hand firmly across the table. Roy was staring, almost impolitely, at the cheekbones and the set of her eyes. She gave him a quick but easy smile—Tanya again, when she knew the answer.

"And how is she going?"

"Tanya's one of the better ones. I think I could say that, Mrs Volska." He seemed for a moment, even at this distance, to be influenced by Tanya's own sense of humour. "When she's switched on anyway."

"Switched on?" said Mrs Volska, with just the trace of an accent.

"I mean." said Roy, "she does have a pretty wide range of interests, as far as I . . ."

"Well, I like to give her plenty of freedom, you know.

There are just the two of us now and I know what it can do if you're, what do you say? overprotective. In Poland, for instance . . ."

"No," said Roy. "I just meant that she can sometimes get distracted. She's always got something to say."

"Oh, she always has something to say," said Mrs Volska with a smile. "We girls have to speak up for ourselves. I've taught her that much, I hope."

"No worries on that score," said Roy. "Nor on any other really. She's doing okay in the tests." He started to turn through his mark book. "Sixteen out of twenty, seventeen out of twenty. Very good in class discussion too. It's not a bad class really. There are a couple of others too . . ."

"You mean that Hamilton Jack, I suppose," she said with a look which seemed to imply he need not continue. "He's a clever boy. Though Tanya beats him at Mathematics and English, I know." She looked up briefly towards the ceiling and the fluorescent lighting fell full on her upturned face. There were lines and a certain dryness there but the contours had survived admirably. "He's a bit . . . narrow, though. Charming, yes. But narrow."

Roy looked away but only so that he could look back again. It was as if time had suddenly escaped them and Tanya was sitting there herself with another twenty-five years on the clock. Mrs Volska continued: "Of course, I don't intervene in these things. That is a sure way to . . ."

"Yes," said Roy. "I think that's right."

"Yes, we are pretty close, Tanya and I. We talk about things, you know . . ." Suddenly she looked Roy in the eye. "The point is she is doing okay with you. No worries?"

"No worries," said Roy, adding a little breadth to his accent. "No worries at all about Tanya."

63

"It has been nice to meet you, Mr Porter." She stood up and shook his hand. "Thank you."

"Goodnight, Mrs Volska." Roy slid back into his plastic seat and watched her fade across the room. He'd seen that walk before too. Preceding him narrowly into a classroom. He tasted the coffee and found it cold. He looked off to the left and noticed that Libby was here after all, over there in the corner, with at least three parents in line. He tried to send her a quick grin but she was too absorbed to catch it. He could see her in profile, talking energetically and with genuine interest. Not quite as striking as Mrs V, he decided, but still attractive in some way she seemed to define for herself. In terms of wine Libby would be a Rutherglen red, Mrs V a chardonnay, something else altogether. For the moment, however, it was Nescafe only and having no other parent in sight he strolled out to the lobby to get himself another cup. P-T Night number ninety-nine. Maybe some celebration was called for. Yeah, he thought, as he proceeded towards the coffee stand. Here's to Tanya. Tanya and Hamilton, come to think of it. Even though he was slow on such things Roy had noticed something happening there. The way she wouldn't let Hamilton get away with anything too pretentious, for instance. She could needle him across a whole classroom just as if she were right beside him ruffling his short black hair. Tanya and Hamilton. Roy and Libby. He shook a new spoon of instant coffee into his cup. And smiled shyly to himself at the parallels.

15

It was one of those high clear winter Sundays, the air still motionless from the early frost though it was half past twelve now and the crowd was beginning to build. There were three or four hundred, Roy guessed, as he finished tightening his snare drum and testing the hi-hat cymbals. The tray of the truck on which the band had set up was tilted slightly. He looked across to the steel flagpole on Parliament House, as if to check the horizon, and admired yet again the way its four supports swept upwards to hold the pole which today, with no wind, seemed strangely naked. And smiled to remember the rumour back in '87 before the opening that there would be a wind machine to keep it flying on such days. Maybe a curtain rod would have done. Today with the Yanks was shaping up a lot better than the one three weeks back with the Russians. A day like this, and only a day like this, could draw Canberrans out of their houses, away from their heating and into the air, as if to kid themselves that autumn had not really gone or spring had come in early for once. It was strange the way the buds on prunus trees or the strange timing of wattles could generate that second illusion.

He heard the pianist's A ring out of an old upright roped to the crossbars up front of the truck. The note had a slightly uncertain feeling as though wavering through all possible cycles that had ever, at any time, around the world been considered A. It was the kind of piano which by definition could not play modern jazz but which for trad had a curious, almost perverse authenticity, implying the music itself had grown from untunable pianos and its polyphony had somehow developed around this core. Certainly Len, who was actually a more than competent pianist in the style of Teddy Wilson, didn't seem to mind as much as he might have done. He hadn't minded too much either when, at Libby's suggestion, Roy had put the hard word on the band to do this benefit prior to their regular gig down the hill at the Yacht Club. Some of the others, the banjo player, Vic Hartmann, for instance, had not been too keen on the no-money angle and a couple had been inclined to question the political aspect till Roy pointed out to them the evenhandedness of the whole vigils project.

"Don't worry, Roy," Jake had said over a beer between sets at the Dickson. "We've played in woolsheds and some pretty sad bloodhouses before this. I reckon we could do a few tunes out in the open air to save the world. What do you reckon, Len?" Len had hesitated a second and put down his glass.

"What about the piano?"

"We'll stick one up on the back of Nick McIntyre's truck the way we did last year for that Canberra Week thing. No problem."

"Might as well borrow his piano then too."

"If you don't mind," said Jake. "It's a bit of an old joanna."

"She'll be right," said Len with a grin. "Good enough

for you guys. 'Close enough for jazz', as they used to say at the Schoolamusic."

Roy was on his throne now and smiling as he thought of it, at the grandiloquence of that term for the not-much-glorified kitchen stool which had served this purpose for thirty years, and looked out over the heads of the gathering. Like the CIA men and the diplomats, who may or may not have been reading them also from the embassy's high Colonial windows, Roy finally had time to check out the signs on the placards and banners. YANQUIS OUT OF LATIN AMERICA! RUSSKIS OUT OF CENTRAL EUROPE. STOP THE DROP (that was an old one now). SIGN SALT 4! He could see Libby, too, in a little beret and a long blue scarf, almost stylish, moving among the crowd with leaflets and a friend carrying and shaking a yellow plastic bucket. There were still people strolling in from cars they'd parked in other streets, the sidestreets that curved in and out among the embassies here on Yarralumla hill. An occasional police car was humped up on the footpath and there was, Roy knew, a line of police behind him on the lawn near the embassy gate. He could see their faces without looking, the way they tried so hard to be not really there. Would there be a foot tapping somewhere?

"One . . . two . . . one two three four." Roy, half-dreaming, almost missed Jake's count, despite his stamping it out on the boards of the truck. "St Louis Blues". He almost came in swinging instead of with the tango on tom toms that had been mandatory for the last eighty years. "*St Louis woman with that sto'-bought hair/ You wouldna got that man, you wouldna got nowhere.*" No one was singing the words but Roy could hear them anyway from an old Louis Armstrong forty-five he'd owned in the fifties (Velma Middleton on vocal). "*Got the St Louis Blues an' ahm blue as ah kin be,/ Got the*

St Louis Blues an' ahm blue as ah kin be . . ." He was delighting in the incongruity of this music in front of these tasteful, neo-eighteenth century buildings set so neatly into the Canberra skyline. Between the St Louis of W.C. Handy on the one hand, and the Brahman good taste of Boston on the other, was as much connection as between the clean winter lines of Canberra itself and this music of the turbid and swirling Mississippi. It was nicely bizarre to be playing this music back to the people who started it—or at least to the government of the people who started it.

The acoustics were not ideal. The soloists in turn moved up and played into a microphone which would later be used for exhortation and which now gave clarinet, trombone and cornet a kind of thin disembodied prominence which seemed to reel out over car roofs and people, as if they were coming somehow from a different station to the one broadcasting the rhythm section, chugging away quietly behind them. When the whole front line stepped in together for the final two choruses the PA seemed to filter and shake them into a single timbre, the surface crackle of an old seventy-eight.

"Well, we'll just give it back to them with interest," Libby had said when Roy had raised the paradox of jazz at the American embassy protest. "It's bad luck we don't have a balalaika ensemble for the Russians. Maybe we should work on that." Then she'd talked for a while of the sheer contradictions, the way you could have those huge symphony orchestras rattling out the ideas of Shostakovitch or Copland in countries which sat on enough destructive power to vaporise everyone on earth, if suitably targeted.

Sometimes teaching that Cold War unit Roy realised how neatly his own life encapsulated the whole nuclear phenomenon. Born in 1940 his first five years had been spent in the prevailing and happy ignorance of the Manhattan Project and the Los Alamos tests. The next fifty seemed to beat on slowly as the situation grew, appeared to ebb slightly, then built again. He'd not really noticed it at all till university and then only in 1962 as he was just about to leave. After that, for another twenty years, you could almost put it aside. Things had looked a lot better in the late eighties when the Cruise and Pershings were being pulled out of Europe and Gorbachev was offering deals that even Reagan and Bush found hard to refuse. But now you had this sparring again, this run on the bank in Central America and the paradox of "tough guy" Redman, with his Hollywood features, presiding over what was shaping up for an American debacle in her own backyard. "I do not intend to go down in history as the first American president to lose a war," LBJ had said, and decided against another term. Now something similar confronted Redman but at closer range, the ninety miles from Havana to Miami rather than the six thousand from L.A. to Saigon. "Won't be long now," Libby had predicted just before Line Six last Friday. "Congress'll have to let him send them in. United Fruit Company and all that . . ."

But the Stompers were well into "Ja-Da" now and Jake was in the middle of his last chorus playing more adventurously than usual. Normally Jake was content merely to embellish the tune a little around the edges and let his strong tone carry the day but now there was an angularity to the phrasing, a pattern of riffs and spaces that Roy delighted in filling. There was a sense of defiance in it as though this fragile pattern of men and sound set against the hardly less fragile skyline of Capital Hill with its stainless steel outlines and motionless flag were challenging the silent power of the silos, the ubiquitous and deadly leviathans and the satellites peering down and waiting. To Roy at that point, as he took his eight bar solo on the bridge, his playing was making a statement he could make in no other way. And, for the moment, holding up the sky.

16

Cy Goodwin was on the phone and didn't see her at first; then he happened to look around, chewing one wing of his reading glasses. He smiled and nodded her into an armchair as the phone call continued. Libby sat forward on the edge of the chair, regretting slightly having worn her jeans today instead of the blue dress she'd taken off the rack and then put back. Cy Goodwin always wore a tie and generally a coat too, she'd noticed.

"Libby," said Cy expansively, so expansively that she couldn't miss the edge of condescension in it. He had swung around now to face her. "What's the . . .?"

"It's about Roy Porter's transfer, Cy. I know I'm only new here and all that but I feel . . ."

"Yes?"

"Well, it seems a bit unfair, don't you think? Roy's been here all these years. He really likes the place and I understand the numbers . . ."

"Ah, yes, Libby, that's just the problem. That and the present government, I suppose one could say."

"But Roy's classes aren't really that small. I'm sure there are others where . . ."

"Certainly, Libby," he said in a tone which almost

patted her on the shoulder. "But History is the area where students are down overall and that's the worry. And there is that other factor too which the CEO's insisting on."

Other factor? Libby thought. Yeah, such as sheer bloody prejudice and folding up to a crony's whinge more likely. She thought of the memo. Roy had left it on her desk when he'd gone off to class. She'd read it through several times looking for a hole and in the process virtually memorised it.

MEMO:
FROM: Principal
TO: R. Porter
Following the anticipated shortfall in the forthcoming
midyear census it has been necessary in accordance
with the criteria set down to nominate you as a
compulsory transferee in second semester.

The coldness of the tone had stayed with her as much as the words. It was difficult to square that tone with the almost excessive concern the principal was showing her now.

"It used to be different, as you know, Libby. 'Last in, first out'—in which case you yourself, or Annie Lansdown, should I say, would have been the . . ."

"I know. I know, but . . ."

"But?"

"You're sure they're the only reasons?" Cy stared at her without blinking. Libby went on. "There must be someone it's less important to. Roy's been here longer than just about anyone. He's almost a part of the architecture." She winced a little as she said it, realising how sedentary it made him sound, virtually inert. And there were demountable buildings, after all, that could be taken away on trucks when their time was up.

"I'm not sure that's any great recommendation in itself,

Libby," said Cy with rather arch humour. "We could do with some refurbishing anyway."

Libby looked at his face, the hard profile, which despite the fluorescent lighting overhead was silhouetted now by the morning light through the venetians. There was a certain moment she knew when an interview with a principal was definitely over, when it was required that the interviewee say thank you and obediently retreat. She felt that moment arrive and pass. She was into phase two now and felt the initiative slipping away from her like a loose pass on the hockey field all those years ago. Cy eased back in his flexible chair and smiled — thinly.

"It's very nice of you to be so concerned about a colleague, Libby, and you're not even on the branch executive. I had been expecting Fred Sykes, of course, but . . ." His look became owlish. "I understand you've recently become a grandmother?"

"Well, not so very recently," said Libby before his point could quite sink in. "Six months ago in Perth, actually. Christmas time."

"I didn't know there was anything between you and . . . except the Peace movement, of course. I have heard a little about that. A principal is not entirely without informants, you know."

"I don't see what that has to do with . . ." There had been a time, she'd be hard put to say how long ago now, when she'd have gone straight on and let him have it. She could still hear the tone of some of those earlier encounters ringing in her ears and some of the phrases too: "unwarranted invasion of private life", "no relevance to my professional career" etc., but she couldn't go on. A silence hung between them which Cy seemed to savour, though it was hard to tell to what degree with the light so strong behind him. What else could be said? You only got to say it once, in this context at least, and it was obvious she'd muffed it. Fred Sykes might or might not do better, if he did anything at all. She thought briefly of Roy leaning back in a teacher's chair down in B6 listening with friendly scepticism to some student's theory. She could see the ironic half-smile building in Roy's face. "But you've got to admit it, Roy, the Japanese were . . ."

Just as Libby was getting up to leave the phone rang again. Cy Goodwin swung around back to his desk and picked it up. "Goodwin. Ah, yes, Terry, yes . . ." The voice in the earpiece rustled on confidentially as Libby backed away towards the door. She paused a moment, waved and found herself almost smiling for having taken up so much of his time. Goodwin, still on the phone, turned towards her and grinned — like one who has stumbled on a conspiracy but magnanimously agrees to forget it.

17

"And now to repeat the main points: the earthquake toll in Yugoslavia set to rise to seven hundred; American president Redman denounces the new United Front Government of Costa Rica; Australian road toll figures the lowest per capita for a decade. This is Robert Winner signing off for National News."

Roy stooped forward, almost spilling his beer, and hit the switch just as some perky cartoon rooster was starting to peck the ground and announce in a West Virginia voiceover "Some folks do say that times is tough but I say you get yourself round here to the Colonel's now. It ain't tough here. It's downright tender."

The chicken vanished into a free-wheeling satellite which in turn vanished into the ABC logo. The soundtrack, a synthesised version of "Advance Australia Fair", ended in a crackle of audio-visual fireworks which culminated cleverly in the six stars of the Southern Cross. Roy settled back in an old armchair, reminding himself to check the griller.

"On the lawn behind me just four hours ago the helicopter which delivered ex-President Ferrerro of Costa Rica to the White House from nearby Arlington field landed amidst tight security." It was Richard Redding, Roy noticed, one of the more breathless ones. "No doubt by now you will have heard the contents of that speech but analysts here are saying now that President Redman has backed up about as far as he can go. Last night's hotline call to Soviet Chairman Andreyev is taken to be one indication of this." Roy savoured the last mouthful of light ale and remembered when the hotline was first connected. It was one of his favourite questions in class to sort out the inattentive. "Marines at bases in Florida and South Carolina are understood to be on second stage alert. President Redman in the office behind me is known to be meeting tonight with his top security advisers."

Roy flicked the youthful, seriously smiling head away and went back to the kitchen where his two frozen chops were now almost burning. The peas, too, were overdone but this was not the first time; the little boiled potatoes had long since split their jackets. He carried the steaming plate back into the main room, a new can of light beer in the other hand, and then left them sitting on the dining table while he walked across the living room, stooped to the record player, flipped a record over neatly, and then walked back to his meal listening to the opening bars of Lee Morgan's "A Night in Tunisia", the interweaving of trumpet and baritone sax implying the spectrum of all that was between them. "*Un soir en Tunise*" as Dizzy Gillespie said smokily somewhere on another track he couldn't quite place now. This whole Costa Rica business was confusing. Hadn't it virtually been a democracy anyway? Maybe there was an element of truth in what Redman had been saying. His brain switched back to the music and was still disconcerted at the way Morgan took the tune at only three–quarters of the original tempo. Generally the later recordings of classics speeded things up but the trumpeter here seemed to be seeing something even earlier than the original. He remembered Art Blakey saying in an intro somewhere how he'd been there when Dizzy composed it "on a garbage tin lid". Morgan had started out in Dizzy's band after all. Maybe they'd played it like that back there in the clubs sometimes. Where had he read all that stuff about Costa Rica? *Time Magazine*, probably, or the *Bulletin*. There wasn't much talk about it in what he knew of the Left. Costa Rica didn't seem to fit their analysis very well. Fred Sykes, for instance, had never mentioned it. Not that he was Left any more. It was a bit of a lacuna with Libby too, sharp as she was, and no doubt sitting down to something similar over there at Kingston, though indisputably more original and better cooked. He looked across to the uncleared ashes of the fireplace, remembering the talks they'd had in its warmth. Maybe later he'd light it up anyway. Turning now to concentrate on his chop, he relished again the effortless way Philly Joe Jones effected the change from Afro-Cuban mambo to straight four for the Bobby Timmons piano solo. Costa Rica, eh? Maybe the mambo was pretty big over there too. Or used to be.

18

"How about Grande's for lunch then?" Roy had said over the phone, having noticed, as he shuffled out in his slippers for the papers, how the frost had already lifted off the ground and the sun had a promise of real warmth in it. As on that Sunday a couple of weeks back at the American embassy, it was clearly a day to be out in the weather. "And a ride around the lake afterwards. What do you reckon?"

"Sounds great, Roy. See you about one then. Yeah, at Grande's. Bye." Though Roy never thought of himself as a romantic he could still remember those few inconsequential words hours later at Manuka between the big plane trees as he sat down at a table in the cool sun and waited for her to appear. Cycling was now the only physical thing that Roy could be bothered with. Playing the drums and sex were physical, yes, but neither of these had quite received their proper attention in recent years. To practise on the kit required an extra unpacking and packing of drums and a practice pad sufficed to maintain a certain litheness in the wrists which, for trad, was hardly necessary anyway. Independence of the left hand was not something highly prized by the Southside

City Stompers. Too much busyness with that could be almost subversive. "You all jest hang onto that beat, Roy baby. We don' need none o' that there fancy stuff here in de Stompers, man." So Jake had suggested to him in an ironic mushmouth not long after Roy had joined the band and still thought himself something of a modernist.

As for sex, that had been pretty lean even in the last few years before the marriage ended. And since the split with Betty had coincided with the first real onset of the AIDS scare his natural diffidence was overwhelmingly reinforced by what was clearly good sense. For Roy, a film of friendly latex between oneself and the Grim Reaper was altogether too fine a margin. There were women who, like him, were on their second or third go round but by leaving parties early, by not going at all, or by not starting anything when you got there, it all very quickly became surprisingly inessential. Which made it even more ironic in retrospect that Roy's one early, almost involuntary, philander in the first years of his marriage had supposedly been a major cause of the breakup. Or that, at least, was Betty's angle.

To judge from Libby's caution so far, sex was not at the top of her agenda either; though there would have been times, Roy could see, back in the sixties and seventies when her earthiness would have landed her under a number of different continental quilts, in flight from the Canberra winter. He could still hear something of that in her voice and see it in the way she swallowed a glass of wine. There was a time when to have gone this far in a friendship, a "relationship", and not to have been to bed would have seemed perverse, even unnatural. One of the best things about Libby was this relaxation, this sense of personal time, a sense that all things necessary would be reached in the end.

79

It was the feeling he had now too as they rode away from the lights at Telopea Park and out onto the cycle path round the lake. The stillness of the day ensured that a sheen of indigo replaced the khaki that normally seemed to rise from the bottom if there were more than two knots of wind. The foreshores were still green, the willows bare, the concrete of the Kings Avenue Bridge and the carillon behind it almost white in the pure winter light. There were other cyclists too and quite a few elderly couples whom Roy liked to think of as European, northern European, out for their Sunday walk and their ration of sun, "so hard to get these days in Brussels or Munich".

He coasted along behind Libby admiring the generous and solid way her bottom rested on the seat. Substantial, but not fat. He was glad to see too that she wore jeans and, like women rather younger than she, would not be palmed off with a "ladies" bike. Dresses were for restaurants (and interviews with principals?) but not for out here in the air.

"Hey, come on, you slacker!" she called, turning back. "Not hard to see you don't get enough exercise."

Roy smiled. "Okay, okay. So we're not all health freaks. Who cares?" But he accelerated anyway and in a few seconds was cruising illegally along beside her.

"How's that old boneshaker of yours going anyway?" she asked.

"Oh, not too bad. It's probably as old as I am."

"Geez, we better stop then. That's a very dangerous age." Roy grinned and cut back in front of her. Maybe it *was* as old as he was. It was probably twenty years old already when he bought it twenty years ago. A Raleigh tourer, strong-framed, robust, three gears and straight, old-fashioned handlebars not much removed from those that surmounted the penny farthings. Betty and he, and then young Ricky, used to go out on autumn and spring

80

rides not long after the government started putting in these cycle paths back in the seventies. Now, despite Quarry and his cutbacks and the advent of local government, these tracks still wove and circled in and around the more rewarding parts of the city—the parks, the lake, the strips between suburbs. Some enthusiasts even used them for cycling to work but Roy had never quite taken things that far. It was okay for Libby, she lived at Kingston.

They strained up the slope to Kings Avenue Bridge then rode on around to the look-out at the bottom of Anzac Parade. "You want to take a spell here, Libby?" said Roy, resting his bike against the concrete wall. "Don't want to overdo it at my age, you know." Libby smiled an indulgent okay and they leaned together against the wall, looking across the lake towards the two parliament houses, the old white wedding cake and the new subterranean one, already seven years in use.

"What do you reckon old Burley Griffin would've thought, eh?"

"Didn't he want it on Camp Hill? Would have been less grand though, I suppose." Libby turned towards him and smiled. "I don't think he'd complain too much if he could see how things have turned out."

"I reckon he'd be happy enough," said Roy, feeling a distinctly geometric satisfaction at standing on the exact line which bisected the city's triangle—the parliament of a whole country at the apex and the memorial to its dead of eight wars midway along the base. "It really irritates me the way people go on about Canberra being too planned." Roy felt himself giving way to an occasional urge to pontificate. "My brother, for instance, came to Canberra once and all he could talk about was how the gum trees were planted in rows. There's no reason not to have an avenue of gums. If a boulevard of elms is good enough for Paris, an avenue of gums is good enough for us. What do you reckon?" He looked to Libby and smiled at his patriotism.

"Yeah," said Libby, taking up the mood. "Why not an avenue of the noble eucalypt?" That was another thing he liked about Libby. She didn't just disagree for the sake of it. Perhaps she would if she ever got married again (it seemed to go with the condition) but "so far, so good" he was relieved to see.

"And the idea that development by misadventure actually gives a city soul when it's all just the result of one shady mayor succeeding another. Take Sydney, for instance. That's pure sharkery, nothing else. Goes right back to Major Johnston and the New South Wales Corps probably. The guy who overthrew Bligh." Roy shook her playfully by the shoulder wondering at her silence. "But you're only an English teacher anyway."

She smiled like someone who misses the punchline but feels bound to smile anyway. He thought he might have offended her, or worse, bored her. "What's wrong? I was only kidding you know."

"I was just looking at ground zero. Right there over the flagpole. Two kilometres up for greatest effect."

"Yeah, I was thinking the same thing over at the embassy the other day. Makes a nice target. You can just imagine some very serious Russian colonel tapping in the coordinates. Probably about thirty years ago. They've had a few spares for quite a while now. Not that anyone's done much since to make them change the program." Libby started to pull her bike away from the wall as if ready to go.

"I wonder how many women colonels there are in the Russian missile force," she said. "Or in the American one, for that matter. A few, I suppose. There are always a few."

82

"Not to mention all the others encouraging little Johnny or little Ivan to get a better mark in rocketry and ballistics. 'Women of England Say Go', as it were. The modern white feather." He didn't quite know whether he was digging mildly at her simplifications or giving way to his own.

"Okay. Okay. I know it's never that easy, but . . ." Libby deftly swung a leg over her bike. "C'mon," she said. "You might as well save all that for the vigil tomorrow. Today is today is today. Okay? As Gertrude Stein would have said."

They cruised off down into Commonwealth Park where the spout for once was jetting upwards, briefly released from Quarry's cuts or turned on, perhaps, for Japanese tourists. On such a windless day it was falling gracefully and redundantly back on itself. On less perfect days there would often be a rainbow, hanging its obscure promise in a veil of spray.

19

Sounds a bit pathetic if you ask me, Fred. You wouldn't've let it go five years ago.

There's no option, Jeannie. Cy Goodwin's really got it in for him. He's gone on both counts.

What? The needs of the school and . . .?

And the seven year rule.

He's not the only one in that position, is he?

No, but . . .

But that's only the Authority's policy. The Federation doesn't accept it, does it?

Well, we've nearly always accepted the formula one way or another. There's no real way round that. But the seven year rule . . .

Yeah, the seven year rule.

We accepted that back in '89, if you remember, along with a few other things. I spoke against it at the time. I told them about the power it was going to give the principals but . . .

And what about this guy? Roy whatsisname? Roy . . . Porter. Do I know him?

You sat next to him the staff dinner a few weeks back.

You remember. Grey hair, beard, bit of a paunch. About fifty-five or so.

Ah yeah. It's coming back to me now. With that Libby woman. Sort of sixties chick. Gave me a bit of an earbashing about jazz at one stage. Yeah, I asked him what he did, you know, as well as teaching and the next thing I got was a whole history of jazz—trad, swing, modern, avant garde, the lot.

Yeah, that'd be Roy Porter. He's normally pretty quiet but once he gets going . . .

I thought you said he was okay, union-wise.

Well, he is and he isn't. Always goes out on strike, or used to when the executive was still prepared to call one. He's not a scab, I'll give him that but he's a bit pissweak all the same. Doesn't like to face things front on. Always looking for a way round things. You know, the gutless amendment type.

Sounds a bit like someone else I know these days.

Shut up, Jeannie.

Bit touchy, eh?

Well, there's no point, is there? We couldn't win. They wouldn't even go out at Barton let alone in the whole system. Those days are gone.

Still you could at least put him on the agenda just to show you're interested. Then if it dies, it dies. So be it.

Well, what's he ever done for the Federation anyway, Jeannie? Paid his dues, I suppose, like the rest of us but that's about it. He's more interested in his bloody drums half the time and—what are they called?—the Southside City Stompers. That's the name of the game there. Moonlighting. But I'll bet he's not in the musos' union, the bastard.

The musos' union! It's even weaker than ours if it comes to that. They'd play for free beer given half a chance.

Yeah, well that might have been the case in your time when you used to do that singing of yours but you can't tell me with all these Class fours and History teachers strumming their banjos round the place they're not doing a full-time guy out of a . . .

Or woman.

What?

Or woman.

Okay. Or woman. But that's not the point. The point is that it would be totally bloody quixotic to fight on this one and "good old nice guy" Roy Porter is just not worth that kind of a gesture.

So you'll just pretend the whole thing isn't happening, eh?

He can always raise it under Any Other Business. No harm in that, I suppose.

Yeah, and I know what that means. At our branch anyway. Three minutes to go to the end of lunchtime otherwise it's a stop work. Should do him a lot of good.

Get it out of his system for one thing. He doesn't deserve any more than that, Jeannie. And it wouldn't do any good anyway.

That seems to be a bit of a slogan of yours, Fred, this last year or two. You used to be . . .

Yeah, I used to be a lot of things but now . . .

"It wouldn't do any good anyway".

In this case that is just about it, so why don't you give it a rest, eh? I've had just about enough at school each day as it is without this bloody show trial when I get home as well.

The poor darling.

Yeah, well . . .

Never you mind. Poor little Freddie. Did you have a nice day at school today, darling? Or did the big boys pick on you again?

Why don't you just shut up for a change, Jeannie. It's very bloody easy to criticise. You're not exactly a Trotskyite yourself, if it comes to that.

"Wouldn't do any good anyway".

Right. So shut up about it. Okay?

Okay. Just for now. Just this once. If you ask nicely. I'll . . .

20

"'The war has developed not necessarily to Japan's advantage'," said Roy, glancing down at the text in front of him — Richard M. Storry, *A History of Modern Japan*. "Who said that?"

"Emperor Hirohito," said Angela.

"August 10," said Hamilton Jack who had somehow managed Monday morning. "Just after the second bomb."

"Right," said Roy and paused for a moment, looking around the room. It was still cool though definitely warming up now. The janitor had obviously been late to switch on the boiler. The coolness gave an edge to the discussion, a desire to get on with it. Though Hamilton had made it the frost had kept quite a few others in bed; Anne Marie and Dusanka, for a start.

"Now there are two questions which obviously come up at this point. At least two. How important was the bomb in ending the war and did the bomb need to be dropped at all? Historians have been debating these questions for half a century now and there's still no real agreement. What about on the issue of whether it really ended the war?"

"It would have ended a lot sooner if the Americans

had given a guarantee about the emperor," said Scott.

"Or just said what they were finally going to do with him anyway," said Tanya.

"You mean to 'demystify' him, as it were?"

"Yes," said Tanya, continuing. "It's not quite as bad as being hanged anyway or kept on ice like Rudolf Hess." Roy noticed her glance just slightly across at Hamilton to see if the remark had sunk in.

"No doubt about that," said Roy, "but that doesn't quite answer the question of how important it was in ending the war."

"Well, there was that small problem of the Russians, if that's what you mean, Roy," said Hamilton Jack in the left hand corner.

"Yeah? You mean?"

"The small matter of their declaring war on Japan between the two bombs. Better to surrender to Uncle Sam than Uncle Joe, I suspect. They'd already seen the preview of that one in Central Europe. Perhaps Uncle Sam would be a little more . . . forgiving? . . . of the *zaibatsu*, anyway."

"So you reckon it would've happened without the bomb then? The Russian declaration was enough?"

"I didn't quite say that, Roy. You know what I mean."

"Well, what do we say then? What do you say, Tanya? Tanya had momentarily lost the drift, slipped off the edge; into some reverie of last weekend, perhaps. Tanya had very busy weekends, Roy knew that much.

"What?"

"What do we finally say about the argument that the atomic bombs on Hiroshima and Nagasaki were responsible for ending the war?" He smiled at her tolerantly. It was easy to be tolerant of good looks. "And don't say 'which war'."

"Don't be nasty now, Roy. Just because I . . ."

89

"Well, what do you say?"

"Well, it's obviously a matter of both factors—the Russians *and* the bomb. Fifty-fifty. Sixty-forty, maybe."

"Which way?"

"The bomb, I'd say."

"Ah, come on, Tanya," said Hamilton Jack, as if they might have been on either side of a kitchen table after too much wine. "Sixty-forty the other way more likely. Tokyo was already devastated by ordinary bombing but that wasn't enough to get them up on the USS *Missouri* with fountain pen in hand. Took the Russkis to do that, I reckon. The idea of comrades and commissars in Mitsubishi head office was not a pleasant prospect, I'd suggest. Not to mention the gulags."

"Okay, okay," said Roy. "We'll agree to disagree then. What about that other question?"

"What other question?" said Tanya.

"The question of whether it needed to be dropped at all."

"Oh *that*," said Hamilton Jack. "There's no argument about that any more is there?" Roy smiled but it was partly a wince. Sometimes Hamilton was just too brash. Had he read something last night which finally settled it then? Could be.

"Well, there has till now, anyway," said Roy.

"But it's pretty obvious they could have dropped it in an unpopulated area."

"Wouldn't that have rather wasted the lesson?" said Roy. "To vaporise rice fields is not quite so convincing as vaporising people. They needed a fresh, undamaged city and there weren't too many of them left by then."

"Yeah, but the Americans knew the Russians were going to come in three months after Potsdam, right? That would probably have been enough anyway."

"That's just it, isn't it? 'Now I've got a hammer on

those Russkis', as Truman said at that very conference."

"Maybe he should have dropped it on *them*," said Tanya, impatient at the exclusive dialogues which so often developed between Roy and Hamilton.

"Well, in a way, he did drop it on them," said Roy. "Though I don't suppose they took much notice judging from the way they behaved from '45 to '49 when they finally got their own model."

"Well, it was only another weapon, after all," said Tanya. "They'd used everything they'd developed up to that point, why not use the new one too."

"I don't know about that," said Angela Marsden in her slightly high voice, as if she'd suddenly remembered that class contribution was worth ten per cent. "Two thousand times more powerful. That's quite a difference really."

"So what do we conclude then?" said Roy looking around the room which was two-thirds empty. It was, of course, a small class. Cy Goodwin was aware of that too but even so it was mildly depressing. A cold morning would only go so far as explanation. What was it old Smithy had been saying before he retired? *You did your best teaching in your thirties; after that it was all downhill.* But Roy nevertheless began to flick again through the other factors ending the war, as if he were reading them off an overhead projection at the back of the room. "Nobody's mentioned Iwo Jima or Okinawa yet and the thousands of American boys who would have been killed in an attack on the mainland." Again he looked around the room and went on. "Two hundred thousand Japanese civilians or two hundred thousand American servicemen? Maybe it's as simple as that in the long run. Which would you prefer if you were American president?"

There was no answer. "That reminds me," Roy continued with a half-smile. "We need someone to say

91

a few words on the first assembly next semester. It's the History department's turn to run it and I thought someone might like to talk about Hiroshima with the fiftieth anniversary coming up just then. What about you, Hamilton?"

Hamilton shrugged. He could do it easily, Roy realised, but it wouldn't quite suit his image. He was the commentator, the ironist, not to be caught in naive commitment, however worthy the cause.

"What about you, Tanya? You're pretty good on your feet."

"No way, Roy. You're not getting me up there with a microphone. Maybe you should get one of the ESL students, you know, one of those Japanese exchange students. That might be an idea."

"Well, it is an idea, Tanya, thank you, but I'm not sure a Japanese student would be too keen on . . ." Again Roy looked over the empty chairs. Maybe one of the absentees? "Well, we don't have to decide today, I suppose, but it wouldn't be too hard. Just a few details about the original destruction and the decision to drop it and then maybe something on whether or not it's been responsible for keeping the peace these fifty years as people are inclined to say. Libby Sexton in the English department might be able to help you with that. She's got quite a bit on that aspect."

He saw Tanya smile and say knowingly but silently, "Oh yeah". He couldn't help but smile too; it was pleasurably disconcerting. He leaned back in his chair and glanced backwards over his shoulder at the clock over the blackboard. 9:55. There was a small but general movement of books into bags.

"Well, we'll have to leave it at that for the moment. And anyone who'd like to give that talk just let me know, okay?" Roy started to gather his own books together as the room quickly emptied. Tanya was almost the first out the door. Hamilton was going to be the last.

"Hey, Roy? What's the strength of this rumour you might be leaving. That doesn't sound too good. You're not going to play trad full-time or anything, are you?" Roy looked up into Hamilton's lean but concerned smile.

"No, it's a compulsory transfer. At the end of this semester." It surprised Roy how easily he could talk about it, even to students. He didn't sound much less detached than Fred Sykes. "They reckon we older blokes who've been around a fair while should move on . . . and the History numbers are not quite what they might be." He looked around the empty classroom. "This morning's not too typical, I hope." Then he picked up his books and walked with Hamilton towards the door. "What are you doing here anyway, Hamilton? I thought you usually didn't brother with Mondays? No gig last night, eh?"

"Yeah, right. Looks like the band's gonna split actually. Singer got a better offer. One of the other guys is going up to Sydney. So it's back to the drawing board, or the garage, anyway." They were outside the staffroom door now. "It's our final gig this Thursday night actually. You should come along. Take a break from all that trad stuff."

"Where is it?"

"Tangerine Palace, just down in Phillip there. Altree Court. Starts at eight, more or less."

"They don't let greybeards in, do they? Do you have to be under age to get a drink?"

"They let all sorts of people in, Roy."

"Yeah, I can imagine."

"You should come. Last chance to hear the old Taipan in action before it splits."

"Yeah, well, maybe. Thursday eight o'clock, you reckon? I'll think about it. And bring the ear plugs, eh?"

21

"Any other business?"

Roy looked up at the staffroom clock. Seven minutes till time expired. Then Line Six History. "Yes, Libby?" Fred Sykes looked less than surprised.

"I'd like to move a motion on Roy Porter's transfer."

"You like to read it out?"

" 'That this branch opposes the projected transfer of Roy Porter from Barton College and calls upon executive to initiate system-wide industrial action should this transfer be implemented.' "

"Seconder?" Fred Sykes asked with an edge of scepticism. Roy, sitting on the other side of the room, had been totally surprised by Libby's move. He saw Sally Cowan's hand go up next to Libby.

"Sally Cowan," Fred told the minute secretary beside him.

"You wish to speak to that?" Fred asked as though, being a woman, she might be content merely to test the water.

"Yes, Mr Chairman, I do." Libby got to her feet and, sweeping her gaze right around the forty or so teachers, began. "I'm not perhaps a hundred per cent sure of what

94

Federation policy is on this mid-year census but I am damn sure that what Cy Goodwin's proposing to do in Roy's case is totally unfair. Roy's been at this College longer than any of you. He has terrific rapport with the kids. He's obviously part of the tradition here and I understand he has no desire at all to leave. I know there's something in the Authority policy about teachers who've been in one place for more than seven years but I don't think that means we have to accept it, do we?" She looked, as did Roy, around the gathered faces. There was a universal passivity. Her question was obviously rhetorical. Roy thought she might give up at this point but she pressed on: "And then there's that 'needs of the school' criterion. The History numbers are supposedly down. As far as I can ascertain from the Band Two concerned, they're pretty much as they've always been. There are certainly some other faculties where the numbers aren't any greater. Why should it be Roy who packs his bag for Fisher High." Roy noticed the neutrality of a few faces shift to discomfort—Bill Knowles in the Social Science department, for one. "It seems to me, Mr Chairman, that Roy Porter is being given the shove for no other reason than that he happens not to be a great friend of the principal, so I recommend you vote for this motion which asks Federation council to take the initiative. That implies, of course, that we, as a branch, are willing to support such a call to industrial action."

Libby sat down, slightly flushed and passed the slip of paper with the motion on it along the table to where Fred and the minute secretary sat at the head of the room.

"Seconder wish to speak?" Fred looked back over his shoulder at the clock. "We're just about out of time."

"No," said Sally Cowan. "I think Libby just about said it all. Maybe I would just emphasise what Libby said

95

at the end, that if you support this motion it means you're willing to go out when the time comes and not leave the rest of us high and dry."

"Speaker against?" Fred Sykes looked around the room. It seemed for a moment as though nothing would be said. Then Jessica Myers, one of the Admin Level Twos, called: "Yes, Mr Chairman. I'll say a few words to put things in perspective, as it were." She looked around the room and then started. Roy found himself concentrating more on her brisk, well-tailored clothes than on what she was saying. "We need to remember, I think, that this transfer is completely in line with both Authority and Federation policies. You may wish it weren't but the facts are otherwise. If you support this motion you're asking the Federation executive to act outside its own policy and put itself—and us—out on a limb." She paused and looked around the tables. She was a thin woman, about the same age as Roy, who had got to her position late in life and was disinclined to risk it now, or to risk her credit with Cy. Roy could see that much.

"Now I haven't anything against Roy personally, and neither, I might add, has the principal, despite some of the allegations made here today. Roy Porter, I understand, is a perfectly competent teacher but he does fit the two criteria concerned; he's been here more than seven years and he's in an area where numbers are down. I don't see that we have any choice. He's been nominated in accordance with Authority policy and he has to go. I too wish it were otherwise but it isn't." She offered a tight smile and sat down.

"OK," said Fred Sykes, "now we're just about out of time here. You want the right of reply, Libby?"

"No thanks, Mr Chairman, in view of the time I'll simply note that the motives of the previous speaker will be more than obvious to members and scarcely need any further comment."

Roy was still looking at Jessica Myers, as he heard Libby's closing remarks. It was the sharpest thing he'd ever heard Libby say and it seemed to surprise him almost as much as it surprised Jessica Myers, whose smile flickered out of control before restoring itself. Roy was impressed by the risks Libby had taken on his behalf but he couldn't help noticing in another part of his mind the resentment that some women, even Libby, still felt for those women who had, against all opposition one way or another, clambered up the short but hazardous ladder of their profession. He glanced at Sally Cowan. Probably she'd like to dissociate herself from that last remark. He took a guess at Sally's thoughts. That damn Libby . . . heart's in the right place but why did she have to go and do that? He's a nice enough old guy, but there are limits, you know.

"Right then, I'll put the motion. All those in favour say 'aye'."

There was a scattered collection of half-hearted "ayes" over in the corner near Libby; mostly English teachers, Roy noted.

"Those against?"

There was a firm, almost bored chorus of "nos" from all round the room. Clearly they had classes to get to and this was all getting rather tiresome. Roy sensed their eyes studying him obliquely to test his reaction and felt something not unlike the humiliation that accompanied his failure with that 2E6 class in his first year out, that sense of acute worthlessness. He'd thought himself something of a tradition around here, entitled perhaps to be haphazard in learning the new teachers' names. There had been people farewelled at recess whom he'd hardly even noticed, let alone attached a label to. Maybe he'd followed that old adage he'd picked up in National Service a bit too closely "Always march in the middle rank and never volunteer". They probably thought he was slack, playing away in a jazz band while they were at home marking Maths assignments or French exercises. Maybe he impinged on them as little as they impinged on him — which wasn't much, he now realised. Maybe they're scared of Cy, the mild-mannered tyrant. Cyrus of Persia? They don't want to be next to go. And that Libby, they would be thinking, she's only relieving anyway.

He sat there not moving as the room emptied, aware of their eyes on him as they whisked off to classes. He knew Line Six would be waiting, or most of them anyway. He fiddled with the empty coffee mug and stared down into the reflection at the bottom.

Then Libby sat down suddenly next to him, put an arm over his shoulder and was saying, "Don't you worry, kid. They're a pack of bastards—and bitches, for that matter. We did what we could anyway. And so much for Fred Sykes, leftist extraordinaire. He wouldn't even put us on the agenda."

Roy turned towards her putting a hand on her shoulder, an impulse which turned into a quick hug. "Thanks," he said, "I didn't know you were going to do that. Nice to know you've got one friend anyway."

"Come on, don't be too down. Most of the English and History people voted in favour, and Sally came in to second the motion; I didn't have that part of it lined up actually. Should've, I suppose."

"No, you did well. Thanks a lot, Libby. Maybe Fisher High won't be all that bad. It's just that . . ."

He didn't go on. It was a matter of energy really. He didn't have the energy, the resilience in the stomach, to handle them at that age any more. It'd been fifteen years now since he'd done it—thirty years since the worst of it, like that 2E6. He'd seen his own kid, Ricky, through that age not so long ago. "Put them out in the paddock for a couple of years" had been his joking solution over a beer in the old days. "Just send them out to the paddy fields for a while till they sort themselves out." Kids like that Benny Elwood, for instance. They'd do their best to crucify you, then bounce up years later as though it never happened. "G'day Mr Porter, great solo!" Yeah, great solo. They didn't know anything about drums either. "A perfectly competent solo", as Jessica Myers might say, if she knew anything about drums. There were times these days when even that wouldn't be true but he still got by. At least he never lost count of the bars as he had once or twice in his early days. Thirty-two bars were thirty-two bars; there was no mistake about that. And Fisher High would be Fisher High.

22

With an almost physical effort Roy struggled out of what he had long since come to think of as The Teachers' Dream. It was always the same. The staffroom and the class could vary but always he would be unsuccessfully trying to assemble material for class, always he'd be ten minutes late and getting later, always the contents of the relevant folders would be interfiled with others and always the class would be down the corridor somewhere becoming more chaotic or, if a senior class, more sardonic and ready to depart. The dream inevitably was unresolved, to wake from it never really a solution either.

The clock on his bedside table read 4:49. He could feel the frost lying crisply on the lawn outside. A few dawn birds could be heard dully through the glass. Somewhere at about the same volume a car accelerated up the street. He turned over on his left side. Often these days he woke up with the feeling that his body was an old chaff bag full of bones which pressed against each other of their own weight. To turn over to the other side was to give them a chance to reposition themselves, to rattle through into a different, though equally random, arrangement. He knew however that it was impossible to get to sleep when lying on the left side and also, given the length of time till the alarm, that it would probably be impossible anyway. Soon he found himself simply lying on his back and staring at the ceiling as it moved away slowly from black to grey.

He was in a cocoon of warmth on the left side of the bed, the doona just managing to hold out the frost which he could feel almost within reach outside the window, a white fragile surface right across the city which he once used to run across when, just a few years back, he'd had that short-lived urge for physical fitness. On the right side of the bed was a cold space that had once been Betty. He remembered how in the very early days at such a time they might roll in towards each other and find themselves making love almost without intending it, as though it were just another position for sleep. He remembered the many more years when he would lie awake as now thinking about the day ahead and lying there with an absolute rigidity so as not to break her increasingly brittle sleep. About a year before the end they had used these hours almost solely for recrimination and then it was too late even for that and she was gone altogether.

And so now was Ricky who had slept so long in the next room. Though Betty had never quite put it in so many words, it was as though she had stayed to the end of a promise and then, being released from it by the sheer passage of time, had left. And Ricky with all his "ups and downs" (as his teachers put it) had somehow got hold of a technician's job (part-time) in a Sydney radio station. He might or might not go to university at some stage but with the "user pays" principle being insisted on these days it was likely Ricky's long indifference to organised study would continue some years yet. Roy could remember almost separately the four or five times when Ricky had some up from Sydney for the weekend. The boy in his slowly disappearing awkwardness as a resurrection of the past, of the difficulties he had both experienced and precipitated and, in his growing confidence, a pointer to a future in which Roy could play no significant part. The three hundred kilometres to Sydney were symbolic as well as real. Ricky didn't even bother to write for money now.

5:02. He rolled on to his stomach and inadvertently across to the edge of the cold. The heat in his right side and right leg disappeared into the mattress. He drew back into the warmth but just that touch of the cold had set him thinking again, not this time about the woman who used to fill that space but the woman who might. He thought of her at the Federation meeting and of her run-in with Cy Goodwin. Some, he knew, would think of her as just a loudmouthed, predictable, old-style feminist but they were wrong. He went back over the dinners they'd had and those easy conversations in front of the fire. He wondered at the way they'd both been holding off, not awkwardly but as if they both knew too well already the complications that can multiply in bed. What they had already was fragile and ambiguous. Sex would certainly change it—and possibly end it.

He saw as he ran over such speculations, and over the imagined details of her body, that he was quite probably kidding himself. The AIDS scare had made everyone think at least twice and had led many to conclude that sex was less crucial to psychic health than they'd previously thought. Roy in the last stages of his marriage had found the whole thing dry enough anyway. Even those few impossibly distant times with Sheryl (all that uncharacteristic planning and lying!) were, retrospectively, less and less remarkable and he could still remember that crinkle of resignation in Betty's face under the bed lamp just as he switched it out, no different in essence from the one she displayed when he invariably put the cutlery away in the wrong place from the dishwasher. When Betty finally left he had felt no great compulsion to step out and prove himself, or at least no more than the occasional and suppressible sexual impulse that surfaced from the drinking and laughter that were always a part of trad. There were occasional divorcees who gave him the thought but by the time he'd packed his drums the moment had passed. The lyrics in some of the Stompers' repertoire, their easy double entendre, also raised the possibility but more as ironic commentary than stimulus to imitation. It was as though the new celibacy had arrived for his personal convenience.

He turned over on his right side and finally slipped back into sleep, imagining as he did so the ample shape of Libby butted up against him. He could almost feel its warmth, its reassuring pressure.

"This is the news presented by . . ." Roy swam up slowly from a sleep that could have gone on for hours. That damn clock radio. ". . . The Prime Minister, Mr Quarry, has announced the expulsion of five Soviet Embassy officials for activities inconsistent with their diplomatic status. One is alleged to have arranged extensive funding for one of the country's best known peace groups, the Anti-Nuclear Alliance."

Roy rolled heavily out of bed and shed his pyjamas in the doorway of the bathroom. "Another is alleged to have had subversive relations with American service personnel." He adjusted the shower, ignoring the mould in the grouting and hearing only scattered phrases now. "All five . . . expelled tomorrow . . . Soviet ambassador . . . no comment . . . experts say . . . diplomatic relations . . ." Before reaching for the soap Roy just stood there for half a minute relishing the warmth and pure stasis of it. In a hot shower on a frosty morning it was just possible, with suitable concentration, not to think of anything else, to have a mind as blank as a computer screen waiting patiently for its first character.

23

"I don't know about you, Libby, but I'm getting darn sick of it." The woman put down the mug on an old coffee table, adding one more ring to the hundreds already there. Her face had an almost threatening angularity.

"Yeah," said another woman standing in the doorway to the kitchen. "It's getting a bit hard to see the point." To Libby she looked as if she'd been standing in the doorways of houses in Ainslie all her life.

"It's certainly somewhat predictable," a bearded man with tight metal glasses said from a corner lounge chair. "Not exactly news any more".

"Okay," said Libby, up one end of the long coffee table and therefore a kind of de facto chairperson. "That's all pretty true. But it's the tenacity which counts; it's cumulative; it makes the point gradually. And it deals with that smear that we're only a mob of communist dupes."

"Canberra Peace Group Receives Undisclosed Sum from Foreign Agent—thought to be in the vicinity of 500,000 roubles," intoned the man in the corner. Libby couldn't quite place him though he was clearly an academic of some kind.

105

"Wouldn't that be nice?" said the woman in the kitchen doorway, hefting up a two-year-old daughter who'd been pulling at her knees. Libby smiled, looked down the table and round the living room. The League for Peace monthly meeting. Collective administration.

"Anybody for more coffee?" came a voice from the kitchen.

" 'Speak now or forever hold your peace," said the almost invisible, bespectacled man in the corridor.

"Well, Libby," said the sharp-faced woman. "I'd like to vote formally then, if it's necessary, that we drop it." She looked up at the ceiling, as if she might find there her tone and vocabulary. " 'That in view of its undeniable failure, the strategy of alternate weekly vigils be suspended forthwith.' "

"Could you say that again?" said a small woman at the other end of the coffee table. The mover, staring unseeingly at the ceiling, said it again, word perfect.

"All right," said Libby, after she'd finished. "As you know, we don't normally put things to the vote as such but since in this case we have a motion I might as well . . ."

"Point of order, madam chair," said the man in the corner. "Is there a seconder?"

"Yeah, I'll second it," said the woman in the doorway, with her child burying its face in her neck.

"You wish to speak, Alison?' said Libby.

"Well, only briefly I suppose, just to point out that I think most of us here are damn sick of getting out in all weathers to stand outside those two buildings. I sometimes wonder if those CIA or KGB jerks even know we're there. We're not even outnumbered by the cops any more, for God's sake. It's so bloody forlorn, Libby, let's face it." She paused as if to go on, then decided against it.

"Seconder wish to speak?"

"I think Alison's said it all really, Libby. We're just sick of it, that's all—it's pointless."

"Speaker against?" Libby looked round the silence and then said, "In that case I'll hand over the chair to Nigel, if I may, and say a few words myself."

"Okay, Libby," said Nigel, another academic with a sardonic edge. "Fire away."

"Well, I think it needs to be said again that this was conceived as a long-term strategy when Roy Porter first suggested it back in May."

"And where is the honourable Mr Porter, may I ask?" said Alison. "Conspicuously absent, as usual."

"Order", said Nigel, his voice rising ironically out of an armchair.

"He sent his apologies, as we noted at the beginning of the meeting," said Libby. "Now, as I was saying, it's a long-term strategy. If we give up now it will have proved nothing. You couldn't expect it to work in six weeks, and you probably need to be clear what you mean by 'work' anyway. We can hardly expect Redman or Andreyev to call a press conference and say that owing to the persistent campaign of the League for Peace in Canberra they have finally seen the light and are going to scrap ten subs forthwith. It's a matter of the impact on the consciousness of people right here in Canberra, in Australia, for a start. Perhaps persuading this government to try something other than its 'born again, all the way with LBJ' policy which some of us," and she looked a little sardonically at some of the younger faces in the room, "remember from the Vietnam days."

"Take more than a handful of frozen demonstrators to make that bastard Quarry change his mind," someone called who had previously been silent.

"You could be right about that, Warren," said Libby, not glancing at where the voice had come from, "but

107

there's still the question of what else we can do. Or what else we can do that's practicable. We could go out to Pine Gap again maybe but not all of us are in a position to do that. And if it's a matter of looking forlorn we'd look a damn sight more forlorn out there in the middle of nowhere than here with the whole press gallery keeping an eye on us."

"We haven't seen too much of them lately, either."

"We'd see even less of 'em out there," said Libby. "And, in any case, if you're going to vote against this you'd certainly need to come up with something better yourself. I for one will be interested to see what it is."

"You want the chair back now, Libby?"

"Thanks, Nigel, I'll put Alison's motion then. You want it read again? Okay, Brenda." The small voice at the end of the coffee table rose up and declared:

" 'That in view of its undeniable failure, the strategy of alternating vigils be suspended forthwith'. All those in favour?" There was a scattered, almost weary chorus of "ayes". "Those against?" Silence.

Now that the decision had been taken Libby was almost thankful. It had been the last item on what in the League's collective administration passed for an agenda, and driving home in her little Laser along Wentworth Avenue to Kingston she could feel the steel surface of the lake beside her under the moon. How long did you last if you fell in there during the winter? Thirty-five seconds? Seventy seconds? She'd read it somewhere. The idea of a warm, free Sunday night, perhaps in front of the television, was not unappealing. She wondered what Roy would say. "Gutless" would certainly have been his comment a few weeks back but tonight he was out playing somewhere and in any event he seemed to have drifted away from the idea himself. Maybe even from the League. She'd been the one who'd persuaded him into it, after all. He would have been useful there tonight though, she thought — and wondered ironically whether it had been him or the policy she'd been so keen to defend. As Roy himself had originally said in proposing the vigils, they were "the least you could do". They might prove to be the most as well.

There had been some satisfaction though in simply making the statement whether or not anyone, most notably those two distant and bristling cabals in Moscow and Washington, took any notice. It was a bit like the *Voyager* capsule back in the seventies, still cruising endlessly into interstellar space with its ingenuous earthling salutation. As she shut the door of her car in the car park beside the tower, she looked briefly at the stars, blurred perhaps by the city lights but surprisingly clear even so. How many angels could dance on the head of a pin? Staring outward she felt, in her minuteness, like just such an angel—but her dance, she knew, was rather less assured.

24

Roy must have felt both curious and in sudden need of exercise for on Thursday night at nine, after packing the dishwasher, he suddenly remembered Hamilton's invitation to the last night of Taipan at the Tangerine Palace. It was quite a mild night for July and Roy figured he could conveniently (and beneficially) walk the six or seven blocks down to the Palace in twenty minutes or so, stick his nose in through the door, settle his curiosity about Hamilton (though not the rock scene in general—he was fairly incurious about that) and be back home for an early night. How good a drummer was Hamilton, anyway? Roy knew how the sheer physical wielding and flashing of sticks was bound to impress the uninitiated. You only had to watch the old film clips of Sid Catlett and Jo Jones to realise that the drums were a visual instrument as well as an aural one. Now on the current video clips the younger computerised post punks had rediscovered the same thing and written it larger. Sometimes it'd be a single snare drum centre stage which they'd hammer away at relentlessly; at other times there'd be a pooling of at least two kits with tom toms running down a whole octave. Either way it seemed to impress the crowd and such drummers, he supposed, did keep fairly good time though the click track on recordings had something to do with that.

As he walked out into the windless night and headed downhill towards Melrose Drive, with its spaced gatherings of traffic lights and its stooped street lights, Roy smiled to think how much more difficult it might be to walk back if he ran into someone and decided to stay on for a few drinks. Given his age and interests, and his more recent caution about alcohol, it was not very likely. Thirty years ago, twenty years ago maybe. Perhaps they really wouldn't let him in. Anything was possible in this kind of joint. He walked along briskly now, beside the accelerating and decelerating reaches of traffic, up past the intersection with Hindmarsh and then down into the deserted streets of Phillip, the hardware marts, the tyre discount places, the cheap liquor stores. The area was well-lit but just a little spooky too. He had the whole street to himself now and there was nowhere to run. He was a little relieved therefore when, three blocks away from Altree Court and the Tangerine Palace, he heard the heavy, visceral thud of an electric bass and bass drum pattern. He's got that much right anyway, Roy thought, and began to bear down on the sound. At two hundred metres it was already louder than he'd ever use on a record player and at the top of the stairs, as he paid his money to a painted apparition of indeterminate sex, it was deafening (literally, he knew, but you couldn't tell them). The room was dark but garish at the same time. The band seemed to shatter in and out of existence on a stage at the far end. There was a bar immediately behind him to which he retreated and ordered a bacardi and coke. He remembered this as a mandatory drink from the last time he'd been to such a place back in the seventies. He had to repeat the order a couple of times over the noise but the other apparition behind the bar seemed to know what it was. He/she was probably older than he/she looked. Roy leaned back on the bar which was otherwise deserted and looked across the tables to where Taipan was playing to a small dance floor filled with what looked like a platoon of escapees from an old Jane Fonda fitness tape.

Though Roy could hear Hamilton well enough—it seemed that every drum and cymbal was separately miked—he could see him only in staccato shots which prevented the eye from focusing. The main impression he got from Hamilton's movement and posture was one of detachment. Even ripping off two-bar fills down across the tom toms he was hardly more animated. It was not as hard as he thought it would be to put his face against the one in Line Six History. Detachment and arrogance were close relatives—or could, at least, be mistaken for each other.

It was only as his eyes grew more used to the place that he could finally accept he was thirty years older than anyone else in the room, excluding perhaps those two sprites behind the bar. The room was scattered with tossed heads and laughter and hung with clouds of cigarette smoke which the spotlights seemed to slice physically. He'd just finished his bacardi and had turned to order another when a light hand shook him on the shoulder.

"G'day, Roy! What are you doing here? I didn't know you were a rock fan." It was Tanya; not drunk, just a little loosened with alcohol. She had a kind of European look that tonight came from the pages of Vogue but at other times foreshadowed, Roy thought, the Polish matron she must become. Though when he thought of Mrs V at the P-T night that didn't seem too bad a fate. "Hamilton reckoned the place'd be full of Barton kids but there's only a handful of us. Over at the table near the stage. Why don't you come over?"

"No, thanks, Tanya," Roy said. "I just dropped in to see what they were like. Last night and all that. He's not too bad is he, our Hamilton."

"Not bad, not bad at all," said Tanya, nudging him confidentially with her elbow as she looked along the bar for service. "When you get to know him. Why don't you come over? We won't bite."

"No. I better not. Just dropped in really. Got a few things to do."

"What, over here? In Phillip? Nothing over here except 'The Big O' up the road. 'Ladies of discretion'?" She gave him another nudge with her elbow and took up a couple of red-looking drinks which had arrived by now. She started to head off with them and then turned back. "You sure you won't come?" She smiled again and Roy almost gave in. What was the word they used to use? Groupie. Not Tanya though . . .

"No thanks. Got to go shortly. See you tomorrow then. Third session. Line Six. You better be there. Okay? Bye."

Roy watched her weave away among the tables and off through the shattering light like a series of diminishing photographs. Taipan was still hammering away, seesawing between two chords and the four or five words to go with each. The singer, male, was sweating and prancing, almost damaging his teeth on the microphone, but the words remained obscure, gnomic, the secret name of God, perhaps?

Roy swallowed his second drink fast, almost medicinally, and wondered whether there'd ever been a time when he could have responded to such music. He could remember jiving to "Rock Around the Clock" in 1957, twenty years before this roomful of kids was born, but that at least was rhythm-and-blues, albeit bleached. He could remember "A Hard Day's Night" in the sixties somewhere but at some point four or five years back, when his mind was elsewhere, a kind of plastic minimalism had triumphed. Why not have a drum machine and a loop tape playing just a single pattern? That would serve the purpose pretty much as well as Taipan in purely aural terms. Visually they were an improvement, he supposed, but not dramatically so. Maybe taipans struck at the brain? There was no telling.

In either case it was time to get out of here. The streets at the door were vividly empty of people, monochromatic and almost threatening under their powerful lighting. Then, when he was still less than two blocks away, the music stopped suddenly and he walked on in a new kind of silence edged by the continuous surge into and away from the lights up on the corner of Hindmarsh and Melrose. Maybe at fifty-five you were just too old (too old for what?) but that didn't really explain it though it did, he realised, bring him a little closer to those mouldy figs he so disliked who viewed with identical disdain anything that had happened in jazz from the death of Jelly Roll Morton onwards. Now that was a chastening thought to take yourself home with.

25

Since Roy had bought Betty out of her half of the house seven years back, a privilege he was still paying for, he had ignored the garden as far as possible so that each year it became more and more like those around rented houses, a few shrubs and a strip of old flower bed against the front wall, degraded now to a slightly raised strip of grass. The only difference in Roy's case was a cluster of three trees, a prunus and a pair of silver birches, all of which were competing vigorously, having been planted too close together thirty years before.

It was a fine Sunday morning in early July, the first of the mid-year holidays, and after breakfast and the morning paper Roy found himself almost inadvertently in the garden walking below bare branches and over the frosted grass. It had a damp, combed-down quality, as if it were waiting helplessly for the spring. Why had they ever moved to this four-term year with its wasted fortnight in the heart of Canberra's cold? Lazily, Roy noted a bare outsize rose bush and imagined that he might prune it sometime—a process, in Roy's case, intended primarily to reduce size rather than produce any increase in blooms. It had caused Betty considerably

115

more pain to leave her garden than to leave him and he sometimes liked to imagine this bare, dishevelled residue of it as a kind of half-hearted retaliation, though he knew that if she'd gone out in a coffin instead of a court room it would have been no different. At school sometimes he'd heard teachers bragging at lunch about the size of their tomatoes and the vigor of their zucchinis: it had seemed so foreign to him he'd had to look carefully in their faces to check if they were serious.

The man next door to Roy on the downhill side was such a man, it seemed. From Roy's back door, which opened onto a small deck, Roy had noticed the garden laid out with an almost military rigour. At the moment only spinach and cabbages but last summer there'd been the whole range of what you could buy at the Fyshwick market. He was also a handyman whose hobby was building houses, living in them a while and then reselling them for capital gain. Most of these had been out in the outer reaches of Tuggeranong or Belconnen but now he had bought this double garage, two-storey affair in Lyons and for the last two years, one way or another, had been extending it.

Walking beside the fence, Roy noticed the man working on the engine of a front-end loader. Farther down towards the vegetable garden in what had previously been lawn there was now a hole about three metres deep and roughly the width and breadth of a backyard pool.

"Getting ready for the summer, eh Kurt?" Kurt looked back over his shoulder and smiled, an honest smile, but with an enigmatic turn of the mouth, a veiled intensity in the eyes.

"You could say that, Roy."

"Or more of an investment, maybe?"

"That too, I would say." He finished tightening a nut on what seemed to Roy to be the carburettor. Hard to tell with this heavy machinery. "Yes, one could say that this is an investment for the summer, I suppose."

"You doing it all yourself, then?" said Roy.

"Yes. There is this company down in Melbourne. Been doing a lot of work down there, they say, but I think old Kurt can probably do just as well himself, no?"

Roy leaned on the new wooden fence which Kurt had set between them a few months back and suggested, "Some people reckon they're a bit more trouble than they're worth in Canberra anyway. Only got a six week summer you know."

"I wouldn't say that, Roy. When the time comes it should come in very useful." Roy looked at the hole, the raw sides of clayey yellow soil and tried to imagine the shining tiles that would replace it, the chlorinated blues of processed water, the summer heat that would beat down on it so far off now from this merely curative July sun.

"Looks like a good big one, eh? Do they have a maximum size in the Building Section?"

"No, not really. There are different ideas about that. It is really a matter of how much you can afford. Better to mistake on the safe side, as they say."

"Safe side?"

"It's a matter of depth; a metre of soil, packed down hard or fifty centimetres of concrete."

"To get a seal? I thought they used fibreglass these days."

"No, no. I don't think that would do the trick at all." Kurt paused and stood up. "You interested in this, Roy? Maybe you would like to see my plans. Just come through the building section last week. I give you a look." He walked back inside.

Roy stared at the front-end loader and admired the way it seemed to balance with its scoop up front and its digger at the back. Kurt was back in less than two minutes.

"Here you are, Roy," he said, unrolling a large sheet. "It will be very successful, I think." Roy glanced briefly over the whole sheet—a ground plan and a side elevation of what at first sight looked more like a small house than a swimming pool. Then his eyes dropped away to the bottom left hand corner. There, in neat draughtsman's printing, it said: FALLOUT SHELTER for Mr K. De Verr, 16 Boondarra St, Lyons.

118

26

It was a grey day, a cold afternoon of rain, the residue of what would be pure snow up on Mount Franklin. Roy swung his car in off the street and bounced up into the carport. He reached over the back for his briefcase and stepped in through the back door into the kitchen. It too was cold but not with that primal coldness outside. The sink was still spread with the remnants of breakfast, the bowl with its hardened rim of cereal, the griller with its lining of fat. He went straight on to the living room and turned on the heater. He was about to start back and tackle the kitchen when he decided to turn on the TV instead. Roy only rarely watched television—history programs, jazz programs (not that they were very numerous), current affairs (increasingly), an occasional foreign film on what was left of the SBS network—but today it was the replay of that Four Corners program they'd been talking about in the staffroom. It would almost be finished by now, ten minutes maybe left to run. He sat down in the cold and watched the screen fade up over a reporter's voice he recognised as Andrea McKinnon's. She was one of the pert ones, irritatingly self-confident, Roy always felt. He watched her with a kind of dazed inattention as she walked about the new MIRSKs the Cubans had got from the Russians. "Great name anyway," Libby had said at school. They were halfway between the strategic and the tactical, it seemed, and capable of being nuclear-armed though no one knew if they were or not. There was an interview with President Flores too, a man of about Roy's own age sitting behind a large desk and, despite the braid on his shoulders, looking quite cooperative. There was a sheen of sweat on his face which Roy found hard to square with the coldness all around him in the room. That was one problem they didn't have in Cuba anyway but Flores clearly thought he had quite a few others. He seemed to be mentioning the Bay of Pigs a lot ("Ze Bay of Pigs, no?") and smiling broadly each time he said it. Occasionally he would dust an invisible speck of dandruff off his shoulder. They wound the show up with Andrea McKinnon, star reporter, about to board the plane at Havana and pitching the question of "surgical strikes", a phrase that had always afforded Roy some bitter amusement ("pass the scalpel, nurse"). It was not a phrase that had originated with the AMA, he supposed. But it was a phrase of increasing currency these days. It was more precise, more professional than merely "taking out" or "blowing away". It had the cruel-to-be-kind echoes of cancer surgery.

As the credits began to roll Roy almost derisively pushed the switch and instead of making coffee, walked down the hall to the spare room where he had his drums set up and closed the door behind him. Sitting on his stool now he looked out through the window over the top of his ride cymbal into the late afternoon weather which continued to swirl darkly outside. He leant back on his stool and flicked on an old one-bar radiator. He watched the rain-blurred lines of the houses, streets and gardens on the hill opposite and started in with a straight up-tempo 4/4 pattern on the ride cymbal, snapping his hi-hat on two and four. He started to clip off the fourth beat with a rim shot. Then in the space that this established he began to build a solo, a solo that moved on to the tom toms and slowly spread out over the whole set. It was a music of despair, of anger; by some process of transference it seemed to fill with images of what he'd just seen on the screen—and with the implications of those images. The connections between warfare and percussion went right back, he realised (that drumfire they'd had on the Western Front, for instance) as he gave himself up to the patterns and their own inner logic. It was as if he set them around himself, fortifying himself in this cold house, till he had a feeling of being alone on the planet, looking directly out into space. He was playing right on the edge of his technique now, as well as he ever had or would; it was a satisfaction he could escape into, something with which to defy all that was outside it. He built the solo to a climax then gradually let the densities thin out again to the 4/4 pattern he'd started with. When he finally faded this neatly away into nothing he looked up and out through the window. The wind was still tossing sheets of rain around the backyards like so much washing. In Kurt's backyard what had once been lawn was now a level patch of muddy topsoil impatient for spring suns.

27

Why is it the woman who always ends up taking the initiative? Libby thought in her GP's waiting room. She flipped bemusedly through a *Women's Weekly* and wondered what had happened to the *Cosmo* and *Dolly* of ten or fifteen years back. Recipes, royalty, "How-to-keep-the-one-man-happy" were now the universal themes. Sex as recreation or personal discovery, all those subtle little vanities, had been dusted away under the carpet by a simple virus. They'd vanished like credit in 1929. The age of certified monogamy had arrived, or returned, like the protestant virtues in the 30s. Libby remembered how the new Quarry government had flirted for months with the idea of a national antibodies screening system and abandoned it only on the grounds that it would not really be "small government". There'd been something rather Hitlerian about many of the speeches at that time. In the last shaky days of their marriage Libby and Ned had both thought of taking a test but never quite discussed it. They trusted vaguely and hoped for the best. It was not really the sort of thing you wanted to know. Then, with Katie's departure at eighteen for Sydney, the emptiness in the house had become so tangible that the divorce was under way almost before they realised. Even the property settlement was more or less amicable, a sense of finality drove them to finish it off quickly. The unit in the Kingston tower was a spin-off from Ned's notable readiness to sign and be done with it all. Libby still didn't quite understand how he'd got tired of it (of her?), so abruptly. In the process of bouncing back (not so easily done at forty-five) she'd taken a couple of risks when her taste for good reds had outrun her good sense, but even there she'd managed a condom, her distrust of which went right back to university days as a "freshette". At the time her periods were scattered almost randomly across the year, and a pregnancy would have been somewhat biblical anyway. There was certainly an irony there somewhere.

She flipped on through the pages. *The Pleasures of Fidelity. Original Touches for Blackberry Pies. Mrs John Quarry—First Lady's Personal Hints for Good Housekeeping.* She looked up at the walls. There was an old notice which read: "This is a private medical practice. Please pay at the time of consultation. Does the secretary know you are here?" And another underneath it which said: "Medical Personal Screenings Pty Ltd. Blood tests here. Immediate results. Confidentiality guaranteed." There was a rather chic photo of two hands in linked close-up, male and female, not too old.

Libby shivered and remembered the old public health clinics and outpatients' wards she'd waited in as Medicare was on its final slide. She'd even had the idea that it was unsocialist to insure privately and insist on your own doctor. "By God, I will accept nothing which all cannot have their counterpart of on the same terms", as Walt Whitman had just said in her American Poetry class. Finally she decided that on a salary like hers (not that it was remarkable but it was still above the average wage) she was only filling a place in the queue which might more properly be taken by someone who had no other option. So here she was, and had been for some years. Old Nettlefold was not a bad guy. At least he knew how to make you feel okay (even wise) about false alarms, the little hypochondrias that beset one from time to time. He even affected to be "a man of the world" which suited Libby rather better than the prim disdain she'd met in her twenties.

She looked up over her magazine at the woman opposite who wore tinted glasses and looked drained and edgy. More worried than me, Libby noticed. The idea that she herself, Libby Sexton, could actually be carrying such a disease had that impossibility about it which she could remember death having had for her as a five year old. It may have happened to others but it can't happen to me. "My death's a chance I never will permit", she remembered from a poem somewhere. She had no symptoms yet—but they could, it was known, be fifteen years in arriving. The episodes with those two guys were just on five years back but . . . Once she would have been happy to let it run on indefinitely but now with Roy she felt a warmth, an overall shiver of interest, and a growing sense of something missing. Maybe there was a little bit of that fatal compassion, too. It wasn't good for him to be all alone in that house with that remaindered furniture and no central heating. Though being alone in her Kingston flat was more pleasurable than she'd ever imagined it might be before she got there.

Roy, she suspected, had come to terms with abstinence better than she had. Stepping out of the shower sometimes her body seemed to remember things her mind had almost forgotten. Roy obviously liked her but hardly seemed to care, it seemed, if he went to his grave with "no further fucks", as she'd once have put it back in the sixties. At fifty-five he was hardly one of those urbane, silvertailed paragons in the *Women's Weekly* and she, it was obvious, was not one of the well-shaped aerobic junior matrons who looked upward into their eyes. But her belly and hips were not grotesque and the crowsfeet at her eyes could still retreat a little when she caught herself smiling in a mirror. And who cared really?

If the test was positive that would be the end of it anyway. She thought of that virus slipping in under the guard of her T-cells and slowly destroying them, unnoticed at first, in a pure and brainless malevolence. It was a very simple test these days, very fast too. Modern science had at least got that far anyway.

If the test proved positive old Nettlefold would sit her down and tell her the position, right then and there. If negative, the receptionist would simply hit a button on the computer and print off a statement for the doctor to sign as he stood there and she dug in her purse for the money. Things had been much worse in the eighties when you could wait a whole week for a summons by mail. The test had a failure rate of .01 per cent but so did life generally if it came to that. She wondered, for instance, at what level the epidemiologists might put the risks of this MIRSK business. It was all déjà vu. She remembered back in October '62 listening with her father as the radio told them the Russian ships were turning back after all. She was seventeen and set to have her last exam in the Leaving Certificate that morning. The onrush of relief at having been given a second chance and having known all along that she would be, had come back in diminished and more personal form in surgeries like this ever since, whenever she discovered that the lump, the bleeding, the cervical twinge was merely benign and best left untreated. Maybe life generally was best left untreated. And here she was now without even a pain.

"Miss Sexton?" She looked up from sightlessly flipping through the magazine. Miss Sexton indeed. It made her sound like something retired from the Crimean War. Old Nettlefold, Dr Nettlefold, was standing by the reception desk. He smiled like one of those old-style doctors in the new television commercials and waved her into his room.

28

"Roy Porter." That was always his opening line.

"It's Libby. Who'd you think it was? Didn't get you out of bed, did I?"

"Not quite." It was the holidays but even so . . .

"You remember I said Katie was up this weekend?"

"Yeah. Right." Roy had already got used to the idea of not seeing her till Monday when the new semester started.

"We're going to take a run up to Tidbinbilla. Thought you might like to come."

"You're sure? I don't want to . . ." Maybe one day they could do something similar when Ricky came up. Nostalgia for the family life?

"No worries. No need to bring anything. We'll just grab some bread and a chook on the way over. See you at your place in about half an hour. Okay?"

And now as Roy replayed the conversation they were out past the Cotter, winding through the second-growth pine forest towards Murrays Corner. Roy had never shared the fashionable disapproval of these forests. He liked those serrated horizons and the way they seemed to transform the clouds coming in over them. Out here, as the land rose up towards the mountains, the clouds seemed closer, almost reachable, coming in swiftly over the skyline. But that would be later. At the moment it was still a clear winter morning and Libby was pressing her little Ford Laser faster than necessary into the corners. A rally driver manquée, Roy thought affectionately, and propped himself up with a stiffened arm as they swung into another corner.

In which case Katie in the front seat was the navigator. He stared at her thick, tightly curled black hair and, looking across to Libby's soft blonde-grey mane, wondered where it might have come from. Ned. And that was about all he knew. From the talks in the staffroom and in front of the fire at Lyons he still knew only that Ned had finally been, in some vague way she never quite specified, unsatisfactory. There were quite a few details they'd both held back on—perhaps wisely, Roy thought. Ned was just a casualty somewhere back along the tarmac. Or that was the image Roy had of it when Libby was at the wheel. Cooped in the back seat of the old '83 Laser, Roy began to regret his insistence on letting Katie have the front seat. Katie had offered it but it had been Roy who finally had clambered through into the back. There was a time, decades back, when they might automatically have offered to let him drive. He had suggested his own station wagon soon after their arrival but that too was turned down.

Then as they'd breezed along Hindmarsh and then along Streeton Drive to the Cotter Road he'd run the standard questionnaire with Katie. Yes, she'd been in Sydney three years now and was doing her last year of Fine Arts. Yes, she'd been at school in Canberra. Phillip College, actually. Pretty good, she supposed. Had to get out of Canberra though. You know, if you're brought up here . . .

They rounded a spur of forest that had recently been felled. A bare strip ran up the hillside and let in the sky at the top, a smile with a tooth missing. In that strip there were just a few scrappy saplings left, hardly more than weeds. Roy thought of the pine logs on the timber trucks he saw so often on his way to work, their rough layered bark, the random twigs still hanging despite the severe geometrical lengths. From the basket on the seat beside him rose the smell of a grilled chicken, well stuffed with herbs. He noticed with similar interest the dew on the bottles of Chardonnay he'd remembered in the fridge. Brown Brothers, Milawa, 1993. There were even three proper wine glasses wrapped in real napkins. He was glad to see that Libby also would not be satisfied with perspex. That, too, was something else between them. There were still some rituals which required a true formality.

Later, after an unsuccessful walk through the koala enclosure (all sky, tree crowns and no koalas), they pulled up near a bare knoll and, walking about a hundred metres up its grassy slope, spread out some rugs and a table cloth. Roy stood back and watched the unconscious coordination of mother and daughter. Plates, napkins, glasses, ("You open the wine, Roy"), bread, chicken, thermos.

"You first, Roy. Don't be shy now," Libby said, indicating the meal spread out between them. He made himself a rough chicken sandwich with two big slices of Italian bread.

"Mum says you've been at Barton quite a while," said Katie.

"I guess so. Since 1980 anyway. That's fifteen years."

"Must like it then?"

"Well, not necessarily. But, yes, I do really. The kids are pretty good at that age. Not completely spoiled yet. And, well, past that hormonal business, the puberty bit." Roy had a swift foreshadowing of what the Fisher High playground would be like at recess with its thirteen-year-old boys rolling and tumbling and pulling at each other in a kind of displaced sexuality and the girls of that age with their hitched-up skirts and caustic tongues. But even through such a vision he could sense the daughter's protective investigation. Who is this guy, anyway? Sometimes mothers had to be saved from themselves.

"I don't know how Mum's done it all these years. Teaching really takes it out of you, as far as I can see." She looked briefly at Libby who was staring across the other side of the valley, not really listening. "Wouldn't catch me doing it. Nice quiet job in a basement somewhere, that's what I want."

"Curating?"

"Yeah, that's the next item on the agenda. Part-time probably." She leaned forward and poured herself a swift and generous glass of wine. Roy saw that it was exactly the same movement as Libby's, a full-throated pouring. "Mum says you're a bit of a drummer too." She went on. "What sort of music?"

"Jazz. Trad jazz."

"You should hear him, Katie, he's okay." Libby said, cutting back into the conversation. "The Southside City Stompers. Quite a group, eh Roy?"

Roy smiled. There was such a lift in her voice; you couldn't believe she'd only heard them twice, once at the vigil outside the American embassy, and another time before that when she'd dropped in, curious, at the Yacht Club one Sunday.

130

"Yeah, not bad," said Roy, grinning a little naively at her enthusiasm.

Now all three seemed suddenly to be staring thoughtfully across the gully to where a tall, bare plane tree stood by itself on the next ridge. It was filled with white birds, fat white birds, which seemed to perch there motionless.

"Just look at those cockatoos," said Katie. "I wonder why they just sit there like that."

"Siesta, probably," said Roy, lying back on the rug and feeling the sun work on his face, tingling faintly already with the wine. He had his eyes closed now but could sense Libby and Katie stretched out beside him. The word "womenfolk" came to his mind as he lay there. It was a nice possessive feeling. Reassuring. "Not a bad idea when you think about it, the siesta. Major defect in Australian culture, the forty-minute lunch."

"I reckon," said Libby beside him and he felt her hand come warmly down on his own. He lay in silence there, hearing only the distant whirr of some car halfway down the valley on its way back through still air to Canberra. He was content just to feel the warmth, the rough weathered warmth of Libby's hand and the gentle thrust of the sun on his cheekbones and eyelids. The premonition of Fisher High was in some other, irrelevant dimension— more a matter of belief than fact. The last day of any holiday always had a certain unreality about it, even the winter one. In a mere four billion years, for instance, the sun would swell to a red giant and casually engulf the earth. For the moment however, in July 1995, everything was fine. Or just about.

29

"Yeah, Angela."

"Good on you, Angela."

A scatter of whistles from friends down the front subsided as she stepped up in response to the call from the microphone. There'd been a slight sense of doubt in Jessica Myers' tone as if she didn't really believe she'd got the right name on her clipboard.

"Thank you," said Angela, "thank you," testing her distance from the mike. She wore the standard jeans and sloppy joe, set off with a long black scarf, the stylishness of which seemed to belie the innocent roundness of her face. Roy watched her from a back corner of the gym, across the heads of maybe six hundred students sitting on the floor. He'd meant to look over her ideas for the speech but he was still recovering from her offer to do it at all. She'd come up to him at the end of a session not long after he'd first broached the idea.

"I could do that talk if you haven't got anyone yet." He'd tried not to show his surprise. Certainly Hamilton could have done it (if he would condescend) and possibly Tanya (if she could be serious for long enough). Angela would hardly have been his first choice if class talks were anything to go by. Hers were always thoroughly researched and then presented with absolute flatness— an essay read verbatim to the class. Roy looked at her again now almost expecting her to pull out two pages of A4 and start intoning. When you knew her father it was not easy to predict what she'd say and when he'd mentioned the whole thing to Libby she'd thought Roy had been kidding.

"I've been asked to speak today on Hiroshima," she began, with not even a nervous smile. "Next Sunday at 8:15 on August sixth it will be exactly fifty years since the Japanese city of Hiroshima was destroyed in a few seconds by a single bomb. Sixty thousand people were killed immediately; the same number that Australia lost in the whole of World War One. Another hundred thousand died within the next few weeks of burns or wounds or from radiation sickness. Except for a single building the whole city centre was destroyed. This was the first and, except for the second bomb on Nagasaki, the last time this weapon has been used—so far." She paused and looked out over the audience. There was no sign of a note in her hand.

"For years now students in History classes have debated whether those bombs were necessary to end the war, whether it really was the bomb which ended the war and whether or not the scores of thousands of bombs we now have in the world have been keeping the peace ever since. There may be a connection there somewhere but none of us can be unaware of what it meant to those who were actually there in Hiroshima that morning fifty years ago this Sunday. Not only the lucky ones you might say, who were killed in the first flash or the shock wave that followed it, but those who died more slowly in the months afterwards of radiation sickness." Roy at this point was forced to admit that she was not just a reasonably talented plodder he'd been underrating. She really did understand the whole thing.

"Now," she went on, after another slow look over her audience, "when not only military installations but many of the world's major cities are still targeted by warheads at least a hundred times more powerful, some of us in our History class thought it might be a good idea to have just two minutes' silence next Monday to remember those who died in Hiroshima and reflect just a little on the nuclear situation as it is now. Hands up all those who think that'd be a good idea."

Roy from a far corner watched the hands go up in groups, in little clumps, and then spread until the whole floor was a low field of upraised hands. He felt a displaced sense of satisfaction, as if he himself had somehow produced this result. At another time, he realised, there would have been widespread cheering and good natured guffaws of "yeah, yeah" and maybe some hammering of heels on the floor. Now, it seemed something in Angela's directness and her humility before the facts had won them over. In tone her speech was not so very different from the sporting announcements which had preceded it. Her gaze panned across the whole assembly now as if she were somehow summarising the upraised hands. "Thank you . . . Let's do that then. I don't think the administration will have any problem with that, do you?" She looked sideways at Jessica Myers but seemed not to register the tight smile that Roy knew was the habitual response to such disorderly initiatives. Where would the admin be if things continued like this? Or maybe Ms Myers was just as shocked as he was. "Just before recess then, okay?" Then she walked away from the microphone and rejoined a few friends on the floor down at the front.

And now Jessica Myers was going on about data checks

and the need to ensure that all data held on the computer was accurate. All those Ks of information, Roy could almost see them as separate items, those scores and grades, units completed, units abandoned and the mistakes that would survive there regardless of checks. Maybe the computer didn't make mistakes but programmers and operators most certainly did. As the PA continued resonantly onwards, Roy saw instead a strip of blue water, ninety miles wide, and those computers either side of it waiting and heavy with information, filled with concentric circles and the grids of street plans, comprising somehow the crossed hairs of a telescopic sight.

30

Roy was in the armchair again and Cy Goodwin, in his higher swivel chair, put the phone down and continued, "Yes, Roy, stay of execution, you might say. The CEO's finally decided the move to Fisher isn't on after all. The numbers there don't justify it . . . nor anywhere else, it seems." Roy stared past Cy's face out through the backdrop of venetian blinds to the road a hundred metres off, intermittently alive with the thinned-out traffic of ten a.m. "So we get to keep you after all—at least until the end of the year."

"Mmm," said Roy. "Takes the pressure off anyway." Though he'd never actually had cause to visit Fisher High, Roy could feel it fading already, shrinking down to a kind of dot.

"Yes," smiled Cy, a little abstractedly, "but I wouldn't count on anything." He seemed to meditate a moment, as though on the unpredictability of power—his own, the CEO's . . . Then he turned back to his desk, almost as if the interview were over, or perhaps to conjure a convenient phone call.

Then, suddenly, he turned back to Roy and said in a totally new tone, "Tell me, what *are* you saying to those kids anyway. You History teachers keep a pretty sharp eye. What do you think about all this Cuba business?"

"I thought I was meant to deal only in facts."

Cy smiled again, but only vaguely. "Yes, well . . . You know what I mean. What do you think's going to happen? A re-run of '62 maybe?"

"Could be," said Roy, as the subject itself began to thrust aside his resentment of all Cy had been putting him through, "but it's a lot more dicey now. For Kruschev and Kennedy it was pretty simple. Mutual Assured Destruction, and that was that. Now with these MIRSKs . . ." The unfamiliarity of genuinely talking to Cy did not stop him from pressing on. The logic of the situation imposed its own demands. "These MIRSKs are so borderline. Are they nuclear or not? Are they only for sinking ships? Or are they really offensive?" He looked at the angles of Cy's face and went on in a slight American accent. "*A direct and continuing threat to our great southern cities?*" He stared out through the venetians and dropped the accent. "What did the Russians really sell them?"

"Who knows? But Redman seems to think they're nukes anyway."

"Or says he does," Roy suggested. "You never know what they really think."

"*A continuing and intolerable threat*, something like that, if I remember," said Cy. "But that was a few days ago. Could've changed his mind, I suppose."

Out of the corner of his eye Roy saw Bill Sayers, one of the Admin Level Twos, hover at the door, then go away. There was an increase of movement out in the passage. The clerical assistant from the Home Science department slipped in, started rummaging in a cupboard and putting a jug on.

"He's changed what passes for his mind often enough

before, I reckon," Roy continued, "but there are some extra problems this time."

"Such as?" Cy seemed oblivious to the movements outside and even to the woman making tea.

"Well, the way Flores has got quite a few of the MIRSKs deployed in Havana itself, or right around it anyway. That's just one of them." Roy felt himself opening out a little. Maybe Cy wasn't such a bad guy after all. He'd heard this theory once or twice. "A full-scale invasion is probably out." He felt released, at least from the problem of Fisher High, and went on almost recklessly, overtaken perhaps by his rising sense of freedom. "Redman won't be looking for a replay of the Bay of Pigs. The whole thing's not very well suited to the old keyhole surgery either. That's the phrase, isn't it? 'Surgical strike'. You can almost see the rubber gloves." He went on in a redneck drawl. *"Jest hand me a couple of them there Cherokees. Yeah, that's fine."*

Even with the light through the blinds he could see Cy smile, a grey smile, admittedly, but a genuine and involuntary movement of the facial muscles. Both Bill Sayers and Jessica Myers were in the room now. He could hear them talking softly between themselves and pouring the tea.

Suddenly Cy stood up. "Cup of tea, Roy?"

"Uh? Okay. Thanks," said Roy, levering himself off the edge of the armchair. "Yeah, black with nothing."

Bill Sayers, Level Two Admin, poured it out and handed it to him. Jessica Myers, in her tidy haircut and tailored suit, who clearly would never, on principle, pour the tea, said nevertheless in a reasonably friendly way: "I believe congratulations are in order" and smiled across the top of her cup. "Very good. Good to see old Bernard doesn't get his own way every time, eh, Cy?"

"You're bound to have a win every now and again,"

said Cy. Roy found it impossible to imagine that Cy had really fought for him at all. But no principal likes to lose staff, he realised; that's like an emperor losing a bit of his map to Gauls or Parthians. The conversation ran on without him now, full of meaningful smiles and innuendo. Roy became acutely conscious of his cup and the texture of his biscuit. He could sense the teachers out in the corridor heading for the general staffroom and felt their backward looks landing on his shoulders. Roy Porter? What's he doing in there? Tea with Cy? That's a turnabout now. Condemned man's breakfast, eh? The conversation now consisted almost entirely of unknown names, probably all of whom, Roy surmised, had several square metres of carpet in the Schools Authority but none of whom, to Roy at least, had any sort of face. "Thanks a lot, Cy," he said and started to back away, dumping his cup on top of the cupboard near the door. He hoped he wasn't sounding sycophantic. "It's good news. Thanks a lot." Cy turned sideways for a moment from his two Level Twos and looked at him blankly as if to say "What? . . . Yeah . . . okay" but Roy did not actually hear the words emerge. He stepped backwards into the corridor. It was not so much that he'd forgotten Fisher High. He had never quite believed it possible.

31

And how did he take it, Cy?

Grateful, yes, I think that'd be the word. But not pathetically so. Though if you put the average fifty-five year old college teacher back in front of a high school class you've soon got a case on your hands, I think.

They can't all be that bad.

No, they vary a bit but Fisher is certainly one of the worst. Old Barry out there never was very outstanding. Remember what Percy Harbutt used to say about the inspectors back in New South Wales? They're still getting it wrong, he reckoned, because no matter what the inspectors did you still keep on getting the same percentage of dead wood at every level.

Yes, but Barry came up through the new system, didn't he?

Which just goes to show. Plus ça change. *Isn't that the phrase, dear?*

I still think it's a little rough to railroad people like Roy simply because they happen to have been at the one place a bit too long. Why him rather than anyone else?

Nothing I could do really—that's where the numbers

were down and he'd been there the longest. Simple as that. 'Course he probably is a bit stale. Never a great one for professional development, Roy.

But what about the Southside City Stompers? That'd have to be one kind of professional development.

C'mon, Laura. Be serious. Actually it's pretty bloody amateur, I'm told, though they did win some sort of competition at the jazz convention a few years back apparently.

The kids like him though, don't they? Wasn't Bill, or Jessica, saying that at one stage?

They seem to, but I wouldn't overrate the position. Often hard to tell. His numbers are never too impressive.

Yes, but surely that's not the only . . .

No, but it's definitely a bottom line; the one that counts really, especially with all these cutbacks. No one's too keen on dead wood these days.

What about this Libby? Jessica was saying she's sparked him up quite a bit.

Doubtful quantity, that Libby. Real feminist and . . .

And what's so bad about that?

Old style, you know. Jeans and sandals. Chaff bag dresses. She's led him quite a turn on this peace thing, I think. He's always been a bit political, bit to the left, but she's had him out there every Sunday at those embassies—or did have anyway, till just before the holidays when they seem to have decided it was pointless anyway. I could have told them that.

If they'd asked.

Yes, well . . .

She sounds all right to me though. I've only met her the once but she's not too far off-course if you ask me. Some of the men around that place could use a shake up. Not the same shake up she's given Roy, but . . .

Shake down, you mean.

Don't be so cynical, Cy. They're probably in love for all you know.

That's the rumour. They certainly get through some nattering. Conspiracies probably. Or saving the world. I don't know that she's much of a jazz fan.

You never know, Cy. No kids around. You never know what they might be up to.

You don't think they're old enough to know better? It gets a bit ridiculous eventually.

Does it? I'll remember that.

You know what I mean.

Yeah, I think I probably do. Cy Goodwin's just on forty-nine so look out. How old is Roy exactly?

Fifty-five.

And Libby?

Five or six years younger, I'd guess, though she looks pretty much the same. a bit too much of a good time earlier on, I suspect. They've both got a bit more fat than they need.

Well that's something that could happen to anyone.

Not if you get a good run three times a week and stay off the liquor.

Anyway I'm glad he's staying. Barton wouldn't be quite the same without old Roy, you've got to admit that.

Yeah, I'll admit that maybe—but there's always room for improved performance, isn't there? If not in the class room then on the drums?

Come on, Cy. Give him a chance. You know he's okay—and with this new Libby, who knows? Second lease of life maybe?

Well, till the end of the year anyway. They couldn't place him anywhere else either, this time. Of course this new compulsory retirement they're looking at will be something else again. Who knows what they're working on. People like Roy are very disposable in that regard.

You really think they're . . .?

Blessing in disguise. More time to practise the drums and so on. Something to eke out the pension, maybe.

You know, Cy, you really can be quite intolerable sometimes. Thank God I'm not on your staff.

Don't you risk it, Laura. You stay right where you are. Class nine. Veteran's Affairs. Look after me in my old age, eh? I'll be a veteran by then, I reckon.

Well maybe Roy's a veteran already. You should remember that. Would have been anyway it he'd gone off to Fisher High. Casualty, more likely. Listen, why don't you . . .

Okay, okay. Who is this Roy Porter anyway? Let's just forget him, eh. Why don't you just come around here and . . . mmmmh . . . that's nice . . .

143

32

Normally Roy's mailbox, a slowly collapsing white-painted affair, contained only colour brochures and junk mail of every kind. Some people, he'd noticed, on either side of the street had put up their "No Unauthorised Mail" signs but Roy had never got around to it. Without the relentless attention of supermarkets and department stores his mailbox would have been depressingly bare. The brochures at least gave one the satisfaction of casting them disdainfully into the rubbish tin as you stepped in through the back door, and the pleasure of surmising how many other residents of Lyons would shortly be doing the same thing.

But today as he stooped and struggled with the catch he actually saw a couple of letters buried beneath the brochures. This too happened occasionally but the letters tended to have cellophane windows and the return address of local authorities. Now there were two ordinary envelopes, one typed and the other addressed in a loose handwriting he immediately recognised. It was curiously unformed, so much without style that it virtually had a style of its own. He walked back towards the carport and into the wind as it cut down from Mount Taylor. Still shivering, he strode straight through the kitchen and made for the heater he'd just turned on in the living room. It would be five minutes at least until it began to warm even itself but Roy stood in front of it nevertheless and began to open the first letter.

131 Jackson St

Glebe

Wed August 2

Dear Dad

Sorry it's been so long. I thought I better let you know my new address. We haven't got the phone on yet but if you're down in Sydney any time you could let me know and we could meet up somewhere. There are three of us here all from the technical trainee section. They're both pretty good guys so I guess I've been lucky. It's pretty hard to get any sort of place especially if you're a group. It's more or less clean, or was when we moved in. Should give the cockroaches a run for their money anyway.

I do see a bit of Mum down here but not as much as you'd think since I moved out on my own—not that you'd want to hear all that much about her, I suppose. I can certainly see now why you two split. It's a wonder you kept it up so long really. I hope it wasn't all for "my sake", as they say on television.

The job's pretty good overall. Some days are a bit slack but we're picking up the technical side pretty fast. Night life is mainly the pubs and some of the bands that play on that circuit. Not exactly the Southside City Stompers, eh! Looks like I might get a bit of work on weekends though with a small studio in Glebe here making demo tapes and that sort of thing. No work on the video side yet but it'll come probably.

Must be damn cold up there at the moment. Minus 5 I saw the other night. Better you than me, eh? I've had enough of that place for a while, I reckon. It's good to get out, I can tell you that much.

And that reminds me. I ran into a student of yours the other night at the Waterloo Arms. A drummer. Hamilton someone. He reckons you're quite a teacher. I thought he was a bit of a smartarse but he seemed to know what he was talking about. He was saying something about you and another teacher up there too. Lizzy someone? I think that's what he said. I don't think I ever met her, did I?

Anyway I didn't mean to stickybeak. The main idea was just to let you know my new address. Should be good for six months at least. We've signed up for that long. And we're a pretty law-abiding bunch. So how about a letter some time in the next few months? No excuses. Or call in maybe.

All the best
Rick

Roy put the letter down on the coffee table and felt the heater finally warming the back of his legs. It was surprising how fast kids could fade once they moved out of your immediate worry. That was a nice touch, that "my sake". It certainly hit on why he and Betty had stuck it out so long, neither one willing to concede him to the other. Together and separately they'd agonised about him grade by grade from kindergarten up and watched the teachers' resigned waving of hands at interviews.

The fade, he realised now, had been in two stages—firstly across the valley to Betty's where so much happened during the week and at weekends there'd not been much point in staying home with Dad or following him to the Yacht Club or somewhere else when one could be hanging out with friends. Rick had proved more self-reliant than either he or Betty had anticipated, a quality that had taken him even further away in the second stage, when he moved along with his mother down to Sydney to start the traineeship. This letter, Roy saw, was a souvenir really, like an old photograph from some university ball or a shot from his own schooldays. Affection was there but it was retrospective, "recollected in tranquillity", as Libby had once said about Katie—who, no doubt, was closer to Libby than Rick would ever be to him. That was just the way of the sexes.

He was thinking about Libby then when he opened the second, typewritten, envelope with no return address. There seemed to be no point of origin. Even the franking of the stamp was blurred. At his first glimpse of the letterhead inside, however, the details of the clinic reassembled themselves. Medicaid Personal Services Ltd and that stepping into a small room off the passage and rolling up his sleeve; then the nurse rubbing a little spirits on his forefinger and stabbing the tip. It was all simply to confirm what in the first thirty seconds the nurse had been able to tell him. Not that there was any real risk, he supposed, given his overall disenchantment with the whole thing since (before?) Betty had left. These days, though, it was only fair to have a certificate if . . .

Mr Roydon Porter
14 Boondarra St
Lyons 2606

Dear Mr Porter

This is to confirm that the blood test you took with us on 2.8.95 has shown no signs of the AIDS virus nor of its antibodies. If however you have engaged in high risk activity since the test we cannot, of course, guarantee that

147

you are not now infected. Should you require further tests we trust you will again avail yourself of our facilities at Medicaid Personal Services Ltd.

Yours faithfully
Sally Lewis
Customer Relations

No mention of the two day wait then, Roy noted, remembering the receptionist's mild discomfiture at the computer being "down again". She'd given him an exhausted smile as she looked out over a waiting room full of patients. "Could do you a handwritten one but . . ." "No worries," Roy had said expansively. "Won't need it for a couple of days anyway." He could still feel the outlines of that naive grin on his face, like a boy buying his first condom at the chemist's. Having waited so long to take the test and then again for the results, Roy was unprepared for the lift it gave him simply to see it all printed so clearly in black and white. As he looked up from the letter and out the window the whole scene with its descending and ascending backyards and tiled roofs seemed suddenly to shift into perfect focus and to have an inherent and rational pattern of its own. The heater behind him was filling the whole room with warmth, the atoms of the air were dancing again and a pleasurable shiver tightened the top of his stomach. He walked across the room to the phone.

"953427?"

"Roy."

"Roy?"

"Roy Porter."

"Roy Porter?" Roy was almost about to hang up and dial again when he realised she was joking. "Roy Porter? Who iss diss Roy Porter?"

"C'mon, Libby. Listen, what are you doing for tea tonight? Thought you might like to come over here."

"This is de Roy Porter of fourteena Boonadarra Street, Lie-ons?"

"The same. The one and only."

"Okay. Vell, in zatt case I vill come."

"Great. See you over here about six then."

"Iss gut, Roy. I vill zee you zen. Bye. Bye."

It was four-fifteen. Plenty of time yet. He sat down in an armchair and slit open a copy of *The Canberra Times* he'd not had time to read that morning. *PM BACKS REDMAN "ALL OUT" ON CUBAN MIRSKs.* Roy started on the first paragraph and suddenly felt he didn't need to read further. He got up and went to check the fridge and kitchen cupboards. Fettucine and spinach. And a soft Italian red. There were still a couple of bottles in the cupboard down the hall waiting for a moment sufficiently worthy. "No signs of the AIDS virus nor of its antibodies". Just as bloody well. Bit hard to see how there could have been. Yes, and there was still some gelato in the freezer. He pulled out the spinach from the bottom of the fridge and ran it under the cold water. The days of grilled chops and boiled potatoes were over now. It was always more interesting cooking for two.

33

And finally she'd stayed for breakfast too. Now, half an hour after her little Laser had zipped away backwards down the drive, Roy was turning through the weekend *Herald*, and setting up a second jar of coffee. Normally he'd have been content with "instant" but when he'd walked back inside after seeing Libby off he could smell the freshness of real coffee in the air and began immediately to grind more beans for a second jar. He cleared the old grounds down the sink with a washing-up brush and smiled at the symbolism of it. Now he had the cylinder of thick, resonant liquid in front of him and was about to sink the plunger.

Saturday August 5, 1995. The page one headline was simple enough. *GOVERNMENT PREDICTS INVESTMENT RECOVERY*—that was one you didn't need to read. An on-file item, kept in ready. The governments might change but the story would always be equally useful. Just call it up on screen, change a few names, adjust the date, press "print" and off you went. He turned to page two where the cartoon caught his eye—an ostrich with a large rear end, its head thrust firmly in the sand and a big CND sign on its arse, the old "Make Love Not War" sign from the sixties (or was it the fifties?), a broken cross, two lovers at work with legs spreadeagled. The cartoon scarcely needed a title but some sub editor had given it one anyway. "Peace in Our Time".

In one short downwards movement Roy took all this in and moved onto page three, an article headed *THINK TANK REVIVES LIMITED OPTION THEORY*. His mind slipped sideways, back to the woman who had just driven off and his almost physical memory of the night before. The laughing innuendoes at dinner, her continuing surprise at the way he'd got his simple recipes right and didn't overcook the pasta. "A man who can cook!" she'd said. "Bound to find one sooner or later." It was not really true, they both knew, but he did at least have the simpler principles. He rubbed his hand across his face and beard, smelt the garlic deep in the skin and, despite a recent shower, a rather more nostalgic odour, a sharper, more secret one he had not really thought to smell again.

He tried to concentrate on the print, on terms like "limited exchange", "display of seriousness", "back from the brink". There was something in the second column now about "damage control" and "one for one", "cities of comparable magnitude". One for one? Now what did that mean? He'd never found it this hard to read the Saturday papers before and smiled now to remember the moment after dinner when it had become clear that they were not going to resist any longer what they'd resisted so far and remembered the joke they'd made about "safe sex". "Never been safe, in my experience," said Libby, "even in the old days. Someone's bound to get hurt a little."

"Certainly slowed people down though," Roy had said, splashing some more Italian red into her glass. "Me, anyway." He'd looked at her across the smell of his own glass reminding him of vineyards he'd never visited.

"Didn't slow *you* down though," Roy guessed with a smile.

"Well, there were a couple of years there after Ned left when I was trying to prove something, maybe." She trailed off. "It's all a kind of time bomb really. With a ten or fifteen year countdown."

"Yeah," Roy had said, leaning across the table a little, as if to nuzzle her ear. "I know what you mean. It's not the sort of thing you really want to know. Easier to . . . give it up." Then he'd grinned, a bit sheepishly, feeling fifteen rather than fifty-five. "Till now anyway."

Libby had then got up from the table, reached into the handbag she'd left on a lounge chair and opened a single sheet of paper in front of him on the table. She'd stood behind him and held him lightly by the shoulders as he read it. The letterhead was enough. Roy laughed and pulled her down gently so she was breathing into his left ear.

"Now, that looks a tiny bit familiar. I think I might just have one of those myself down the hall."

Then she'd swung around the chair and sat down sideways on his knees. He rubbed his face against hers without really kissing it.

"Maybe we should just go down there and have a look."

34

It was one of the Saturday afternoon gigs at the Yacht
Club. Despite its being on each week from April to
August, Roy had forgotten it till lunch; drifting at first
through the lazy aftermath of the night before with coffee
and papers; then suddenly and paradoxically deciding
to give the whole place a thorough clean up. Libby would
be back, he didn't doubt that now, and though she was
no more than functionally neat herself Roy had felt a
need to get the place in order, starting with that heavy
shadow of mould in the shower recess. The fact that
this proved almost impossible had not taken the edge
off his mood. About one he'd strolled down to the Lyons
Shoprite and managed to find a reasonable camembert
and a fresh bread stick ("baguette" rather—Betty had
always preferred the French). In a clean house then, albeit
with old furniture, he'd sat in what had seemed,
potentially, a final silence, savouring the last of his
solitude, knowing that it was no longer enforced but
merely an option, an option he knew he'd be happy to
forego if the best of last night could be sustained. He
even swallowed down a half-glass of red they'd left behind
on their way to the bedroom. Despite his usual cords

and jumper, the detectable paunch and his patchy grey hair, Roy, as he sat there reading the paper and looking out over the local rooves, had felt almost stylish, at least in the provincial sense, as though seated perhaps at the "Paris end of Collins Street".

About three he'd packed his drums into the wagon and cruised slowly round to the Yacht Club. A cold front had moved in from the south-west cutting up the lake and sharpening Black Mountain against a sleety grey sky. The car heater, dilatory as usual, had finally come on in Novar Street just in time to emphasise the ache of getting out into the weather and lugging his drums once more across the car park.

Now, well into the third set, the afternoon was almost night. Black Mountain, he could see off to the right there, was just one shade of darkness against another. The crowd was small but strangely attentive, the men holding their middies and staring at the ceiling, the women seeing the band directly and looking as if they might, at any moment, swing on to the dance floor, invited or not. And now it was "Tin Roof Blues"—medium slow. Roy set down a steady four on the big ride cymbal, enjoying the sharp definitive click of a hickory tip on metal. It formed a kind of hardened centre with a copper wash around it. Murray, on bass, was getting his deep, French-polished, European sound. Jake, on cornet, was having one of his really good days. He came into the final chorus with an insistent, almost unbearable triplet figure that so lifted the band he might for a moment have been taking the key up a tone. The pianist felt it too and fed him strong, two-fisted sostenuto chords as the rhythm cut steadily through them.

Roy, who'd earlier been wishing Libby could have heard them on such a good day, had for the moment forgotten her completely as he disappeared into the music.

The drums were the focus; it all started there. A symphony conductor could not have felt more central. A shiver rippled up and down the back of Roy's neck. He could feel it in his spine too. The audience might be out there somewhere but right now there was nothing else but the band. He saw all six as if on the surface of a ruined moon, playing directly into the vacuum, the music transcending the need for air to bear it along and radiating endlessly in all directions out into space.

Sometimes you felt the same thing in recordings, a sudden lift to another level. Whole styles were based on attempts to fake it but when it really happened there was no doubt at all. Often it lasted a few seconds, only rarely more than a couple of choruses; on a good day it could be two or three whole tunes. On many jobs there was no sense of it at all but if you weren't there playing it could never happen. Even as Jake finished and the clarinetist started out over the applause, Roy could feel the moment fading. It might return later, it might not.

Released now, he glanced out into the crowd again as though it had all been suddenly put back in the room. He saw a heavy, sandy-blonde woman whom he momentarily mistook for Libby. Another flicker of adrenalin came up between his shoulder blades and just as quickly disappeared. She'd only heard the band twice and neither time at its best. If she'd heard them just now, he knew it could have told her much more about him than he would ever be able to tell her over a dinner table, or late at night and naked, staring at the ceiling. At one point in bed with her last night, there'd been something similar but that was somehow more provisional, more entangled with the world. The music was purer but this new, rough-edged, more human involvement was no less welcome. As the whole front line came in for the final chorus he was already driving

155

on around the lake, his wagon full of drums, the tape
deck spinning, driving on alone past the old parliament
house (still white at night) to Libby's high flat in its tower
at Kingston.

35

These days, the Venetian, just two blocks away from Libby's Kingston tower, was, for teachers at least, a couple of notches out of range. But Roy was not in a mood to let that worry him. Earlier, over the antipasto, their talk had circled round "that bastard Cy", his motives in trying to get rid of Roy in the first place, the attitude he'd have now the move had fallen through (for the time being anyway) and Jessica Myers's assumption that Cy had somehow prevented it. They laughed a little too over Fred Sykes's implication that his "veiled threat" of industrial action might have had something to do with Roy's reprieve. The bastard hadn't even put it on his agenda. Then it moved on to mutual students like Angela Marsden and how she'd gone so well on that assembly with her Hiroshima talk. "Lot of people wrong about that girl," Roy had insisted. They even amused themselves a little with how their relationship had intrigued the others in the staffroom.

"They just can't make up their tiny minds, Roy," Libby had said. "On the one hand they think we're just too old for it. On the other they can't see any other explanation."

"And now we've proved one half wrong and the other right."

"Or the other way around." Libby looked up and twisted the last green strands of fettucine with her fork. "You know," she said, with her mouth not quite yet empty, "we did take quite a time to get around to . . ."

Roy smiled, "Can't be too cautious. We're the walking wounded, you know, we divorcees."

"Slow but sure, eh?" said Libby, pouring herself some more red and smiling. "Is that quite how you'd describe last night?"

Roy grinned and winced at the same time. "Well, next time maybe." He turned and signalled with the empty bottle toward the waiter.

"Next time?" She went into her German routine. "Vatt do you mean, ze next time?" He gave her leg a jokey rub under the table.

"Like tonight maybe?" He felt so playful he could hardly recognise himself. "No need to risk the boys in blue. Just back to your place, me and you," he rhymed, feeling the Chianti getting to his cheeks. It was a genuine Classico, credit card special, and Roy swirled a last mouthful around on his tongue as the waiter stooped down with a new bottle. It was not, he guessed, on the wine writers' catalogue but it was different from anything in this country and with the exchange rate being what it was the foreignness itself was an instant luxury. There'd been quite a bit of foreignness in the last twenty-four hours, one way or another, and he was looking forward to even more of it. He gazed unselfconsciously at the woman across the table, at the broad face, the blonde-grey hair hanging loosely to the shoulders and, almost rudely, stared into her blue-grey eyes.

"You're very confident tonight," she said. "Don't you

get presumptuous now. Jezebel doesn't approve of strange men."

"Why did you call it that anyway?"

"Her."

"All right, 'her'," said Roy. "That bloody cat's too slack for a name like that. 'Captain Snooze' would be better. Remember those Captain Snooze ads?"

"Thought you never watched the commercials?"

"Must've been a mini-series or something. I used to watch quite a lot of TV at one stage."

"After Betty left?"

"I suppose so. Didn't you?"

"Not me, kid. I was really out and about. Just as well you didn't know me then, eh? Took a little while to realise how much better off I was by myself, actually." Libby leaned over with the bottle and topped up Roy's glass before filling her own. "You guys have got us all psyched up to think you're indispensable. You're not, you know." She must have seen a flicker in his face for she reached over and took up his hand. "Not quite, anyway."

"Well not tonight, I hope," Roy said, as the waiter stooped between them with the veal *campagnola*. The hot strong smell of tomato, garlic and melted cheese invaded their nostrils. Roy thought just once of his little paunch and tucked in. There had been times when, with a woman hovering like this, he would have striven for leanness and, in summer, a tan. But he could see that was all pointless now. "You need something to get your arm around," he remembered Libby saying once in the staffroom when the topic of slimming had arisen yet again. What was the point of thinness anyway? He looked contentedly around the room. The Venetian was very self-contained. Warm with just the right number of customers. The décor matched the food — determined perhaps but not pretentious. There was a scattering of indoor plants but they stopped well short of the greenhouse effect. Then Roy, half-forgetting his food, thought suddenly of what that phrase really meant and how it had receded lately, like all that talk about the ozone layer. Such leisurely and long-term threats had been swept away to non-existence by the crisis in Cuba, the posturing of Redman and Andreyev and all their diminutive clones; Quarry on the one hand, those Warsaw Pact careerists on the other.

"Hey," Libby said, giving him a light kick under the table. "You're not about to drift off on me, are you? What about your *campagnola*?"

"Yeah. Sorry. I was just thinking."

"Thinking what?"

"You know. Bloody Cuba, those MIRSKs in Havana, all that Redman stuff . . ."

"Yeah, well, it's probably been worse. There's not much we can do about them tonight, is there? If there ever was."

"We charged a few windmills though," Roy said. "Not that they paid us any attention."

Libby reached across the table, almost knocking his wine glass over, and said, "Listen Roy, let's just give it a miss. There's nothing we can do, right? Not about that anyway," she smiled and made a vague signal upwards. "Let's just stick to the agenda, eh? Dinner at The Venetian, then later at my place, okay?"

"Okay," said Roy. "Now what about dessert?"

36

As he tried inexpertly to release her breasts Libby wondered in another part of her mind just how many men had attempted that same achievement behind her ribs: a dozen maybe, counting the parked cars of adolescence, discounting the few years there back in the sixties when she'd abandoned a brassiere altogether. She smiled a moment in the half-darkness at the old male myth. They never really became competent. What they couldn't see in front of their eyes was always difficult to handle.

She felt his hands move down the small of her back and cup her buttocks; then once more go back to attempt the clip. His beard tickled gently against her neck and shoulders. The smell too was always a part of it, not so much the alcohol or garlic (no way to smell those when you had them yourself) but the man-smell itself. Not exactly unwashed, though there was certainly some sweat in it somewhere. And certainly it was unprocessed, unmoderated, except just now through sexual excitement. It was a smell you could give up for years at a time but never quite forever. And, of course, it varied; some man smells were downright unacceptable but they wouldn't be getting in this close.

She ran her hands up under his skivvy and jumper, lifting the whole lot over his head. In the light glancing down the passage from the living room she saw that his body was just a bit more overweight than it had seemed last night over at his place. He was a bit hairy, too, but that went with the species; though it was always disconcerting to find it on the back of the shoulders, a bit too close to the ape. "Goats and monkeys," she remembered from the Shakespeare class, "the beast with two backs." There was no one now who would care too much. "Thou has committed—/Fornication but that was in another country/And besides the wench is dead." She breathed his name a few times into his ear to encourage him then stepped easily out of her pants. She felt him pull her up hard, the rim of her pubic bone, that springy hair, butting in against his trousers and the sudden shape there straining to be released. They liked that, she knew—the "*déjeuner sur l'herbe*" syndrome. Men in top hats and everything else, women with their gear off. Aesthetic contemplation. Bullshit. King and courtesan, more likely. She reached down (as Manet's woman should have done) and undid his belt and zipper. In two steps he was naked entirely. Libby stood back from him a moment, smiling and pleased with herself, watching him in the half light. Then he moved in to hug her against him, at the same time succeeding easily now in releasing her bra. She stood there kissing him, all over the chest from the neck to the belly, as though relishing the texture, another course in the meal perhaps, an old wine rediscovered. At the same time she could feel his hands playing her lines from hips to armpit, that inward sweep of the guitar, the full hips of a cello. There was a blurring to that image, she knew, but his hands seemed not to notice. She kissed her way back upwards to his throat. She knew that somewhere there would be complications, the little tradeoffs and daily struggles but she knew too that much of that had been settled already in those quiet lines off in the staffroom and also in those cautious evenings by the fire over at Lyons. "Neo-platonic," as she'd joked to him once. Last night had been a halfway point, objectively a failure but known by both to be inescapable, a kind of first lesson where one must inevitably get things wrong. They were both, however, forgiving teachers and not without humour. Roy, she suspected, had thought she'd be more sardonic, more caustic, but her basic seriousness had surprised even herself. The humour had simply underlined it.

His hands had moved now from that inward curve and were savouring the twin globes of her buttocks. She slipped an almost retributive palm under his scrotum and drew him gently back towards the bed, pulling aside the doona with her free hand and sinking down into the warmth of the electric blanket. She smiled to remember the look she must have had on her face turning it on as they left for the restaurant. As she spread out her legs beneath him she felt the doubled warmth of his weight pressed down on her and the small dependable heat of the wires below her. She felt him rubbing himself luxuriously along her belly and up between her breasts and felt at the same time the electricity beneath her receding endlessly towards the Snowy, the Main Range with its drifts of snow and buried streams. The warmth was total now, above her, below her, outside and inside. She felt her body crying its old familiar wish to be held in such moments for ever.

37

For Cy Goodwin three times each week was the absolute minimum. Get the heart right up to 120 and keep it there for twenty minutes. That was the only way to handle running. Sunday morning was always a good time. It gave one a nice sense of superiority to be running through a whole suburb of people sleeping off the night before, or doing their best to, if blessed with children. At one stage he and Laura had almost adopted one—got as far as the forms anyway—but Laura had gone cold on it finally. Three meetings a week and all that working back were almost enough to make a person grateful for that little problem of Laura's. Three kids and he'd probably still be a Level Two in a high school somewhere trying to find time for some professional reading and wondering why he didn't quite enrol in one of those Ed. Admin. diplomas out at the CAE. Principal at forty-three in a system renowned for its glacial promotions had been doing rather well. No one denied that. It had taken the old-timers at the Principals' Council quite a time to get used to it actually but he'd shown them that Cy Goodwin and Barton College would not be condescended to. Of course, you had to take a tough line with these people sometimes. Those guys would steal your staff and/or students given half a chance with their influence on placement panels and their seemingly ingenuous re-zoning proposals. You had to be tough with your own people, too, at times. That Roy Porter, for instance. He'd had a bit of a shake-up but it'd done him no harm in the end. Too sedentary by far, that lad. People like him could die in their chairs and still take three days to be noticed. That Libby Sexton though, they'd probably notice in her case. The silence. But she was no problem really. Gone at the end of the year when Annie Lansdown came back. Might even have had a good effect. She'd sorted old Roy out anyway.

As he pounded up Beasley Street now with its spec-built European mansions Cy suddenly forgave himself a little and paused to look back across the valley. A heavy mist obscured the white lines of Woden Plaza and lapped around the third or fourth storey of the MLC tower. Five minutes earlier he'd been down there in that cold world himself but now, as he turned and looked uphill, the dried out grass of Mount Taylor was almost golden with dew and the early sun. Though Laura didn't think much of his eye for beauty the shining slope seemed to draw him upwards to where the houses stared confidently out across the valley. He had set off at 7:20 and here now on his wrist, as he slowed to walk up his own drive, it was 7:40. Twenty minutes right on the knocker. He stood for a few seconds checking his pulse with the thumb of his right hand then loped out on the lawn to pick up his paper, disappointed somehow that the dew was not quite frost. Then, in a moment, he was in through the back door and reaching into the fridge for his low fat milk and stooping to a cupboard for muesli. Laura, of course, would still be asleep—more or less, anyway. Best left like that. He'd take her a cup of tea later. He stood near the sink pouring the thin milk onto his muesli: processed bran, rolled wheat, shredded coconut, sultanas, mixed peel, rolled oats . . . He loved its paleness and the legitimate sweetness of it. Good roughage too. He flicked on the transistor which stood on the window sill.

"This is the ABC news. We repeat the message which came in at six o'clock this morning Australian time. Following what is understood to have been an unsuccessful US air strike, American tactical nuclear weapons, assumed to be Cherokees, have made a pre-emptive strike against Cuban MIRSK missiles stationed on the outskirts of Havana." Cy picked up the radio and fine-tuned it, thinking with annoyance even as his mind processed the information, of how his wife had never in twenty years been able to tune a radio properly. He turned up the volume but not enough to carry through to the bedroom. "At the UN Security Council, Ambassador Cherzinsky has made a violent attack on the US action and has said that Russian retaliation for this attack on their ally will be swift and sure and repaid in kind. This has been widely taken to refer to a similar strike to be made against a major American ally, though not necessarily in the American hemisphere." In a kind of daze Cy began filling the jug to make coffee, the noise of the water washing away a few sentences before he heard, " . . . has appealed for calm and states that while the Australian Government supports US actions as being the only possible response to the Cuban provocation he does not think that an Australian city would be singled out. Here is a recording of the Prime Minister's statement . . ."

As he listened to Quarry's apologia and kept on steadily with his muesli, Cy was intrigued by something he couldn't quite bring to focus. Then at last the image sharpened. The Prime Minister's voice, thinned out by radio, had the same involuntary slippage of pitch he'd once heard from a teacher long ago losing control of a high school assembly.

38

Tanya woke up feeling a drift of cold air along her spine. It took her a moment to understand why she was so cramped in her own bed. The lean, smooth back of Hamilton Jack still pushed up hard against her breasts and stomach. She felt the tightening of dried semen on her belly and remembered with a slight shiver how it had got there. Now he'd somehow wrenched her side of the doona across the bed and left her back naked. She drew her arm out from under his neck and gently pulled the doona back across the bed with her left hand. Hamilton gave a slight groan, no more than a murmur, and slept on. Tanya snuggled in tight against the warmth and newness of his body, a slimness that stopped neatly short of being undernourished.

Gina would be coming back from Sydney this afternoon and already Tanya felt an urge to bundle this souvenir of Saturday night out the door. He'd looked pretty cool up there behind all those drums, surrounded by mikes, half-hidden by cymbals and those terraces of tom toms. That hard, nonchalant look, involved but not involved, so much removed from the gyrations of the guitarists and the manic staccato of the keyboardist. Her memory of it was arranged in a series of flashlit stills with Hamilton the only constant. Later, much later, after all his drums had been packed into the new band's wagon and sent off somewhere to be picked up next day, and later again, after the drive in her car (Gina's car) up the long curve of La Perouse Street to Red Hill and this third-floor unit, he'd been, well, a good deal less detached.

She remembered again with a slight smile how they'd slipped through the front door, found the heating on low and trailed straight through to her room, undressing each other in front of the one-bar radiator which had hardly heated up before they were in bed. She could feel again, as she pressed herself lightly against him now, how he'd propped himself above her and rubbed himself tentatively along her belly and how she'd felt enormously older than he was, as though his desire might be a sickness which only she could cure. And later, a little abstractedly, as if remembering some theorem in Maths, he'd brought her gently to a climax with his fingers. "Safe," she'd said. "Got to be safe." And even then, feeling the twinned smoothness of their bodies against each other, she'd thought of those secretions, those fluids and the life (and possibly the death) they would contain for those first few seconds drying on the skin. And managed blankly to hold back a half-minute or so before hugging that flat stomach, those lean legs to her in a kind of immolation.

There was no going back to sleep now. The light was quite strong, the kind of light that on a weekday would have had her stirring for breakfast, shower and nine o'clock Maths. Soon this Sunday would be opening out and requiring her to get the unit back in order, to get this Hamilton out of her bed and, not too obtrusively, out of the building. She could feel her mother's briskness and adventurous good sense beaming up the line already

169

from Sydney. She was tolerant, yes, but not quite this tolerant. Still, there was no great need to hurry; another half-hour would make no difference. Where things might go from here with Hamilton was hard to tell. It was not easy to see how they'd got this far. That ribbing they both went in for had always had an edge of sexual challenge to it. It could be self indulgence too, she had to admit. Some girls thought him incurably pretentious but they hadn't seen him naked in front of that little radiator last night, or she hoped they hadn't. Ann Marie had called him a "heart-breaker" and, seeing how true this could be with no intention on his part, she had, in one way at least, held herself back a little and was surprised at how well she'd managed it. If there was "safe sex" maybe there was "safe love" too. The future would spin out much the same whatever she chose to do about it. Today Year Twelve, tomorrow the world. She propped herself on an elbow and looked at the back of his sleeping head, the clipped black hair. She could see, without even looking, his sleep-filled face on the other side with maybe the trace of a smile. She slipped an arm in under his shoulder, experimentally, as if to see how slowly she could lift him from his dreams.

"Here is the Prime Minister's statement . . ." As the first seven words flicked into her consciousness, Tanya remembered how on the Thursday night she'd set the alarm for 7:55 to make her Friday class at nine and how on Saturday the radio was already going when she'd come back from the train after dropping off her mother. She understood the tone rather than the words, the self-important, "masculine" tone of journalists and politicians all over the world. Did their sex make any difference? "Ladies and gentlemen. As you will already know the world situation in the last few hours, especially in Central America, has seriously . . ." She leant out from the bed

170

and hit the switch with her spare hand. She was remembering something old Roy Porter had said in History just last Friday: "Politicians are only interested in power in the end." "And in the beginning, too," this lovely smart boy in bed beside her had added. And I, at least, have the power not to listen, she reminded herself, taking some joy in putting back the silence. Then she turned back to Hamilton, restless already and coming up from his depths faster than she'd intended.

39

Roy had originally woken up about seven, taken a moment to remember where he was, then propped himself quietly on his elbow. He looked across at Libby where she lay with her back to him, the undulations of her shoulder and hip silhouetted against the diffused light from the window. Though the curtains were drawn he could imagine the view, having seen it from the balcony there in the evening and knowing how the lake would look under mist on such a morning, with the shadowy grey concrete of the Russell Offices and the scrappy eucalypts running up the side of Mount Pleasant and old General Bridges up there in his grave.

Though he knew Libby was a heavy sleeper (she sometimes even missed the ten o'clock deadline at college), he didn't want to risk disturbing her by hauling himself out from under the doona and padding off down the hall to the toilet. He simply lay there resting on his elbow—like a Roman at lunch, he imagined with a smile—and relished once again the old sensation of a woman asleep in bed beside him, the warmth she emanated and the classic outlines under the covers. It was Sunday, he remembered, and there was no hurry.

By the clock on her bedside table it was 6:30. In two hours maybe they would get up to a slow breakfast with coffee and bacon and eggs, and muesli too, with a little stewed fruit. He could smell it already. They would pull back the curtain and watch the last of the mist go up off the lake. They would not say much, not even Libby this time; they would just let the facts of these last two nights sink in . . . and their implications. Later there'd be the question of who'd shift in on whom and who'd sell — or rent. They'd both learned that lesson well enough, always to leave a back door open. Then he realised that that was a habit only. There was no reason why this shouldn't go on for years, for just as long as they had left maybe.

Yes, there was no hurry, no hurry at all. He sank carefully back into the bed and turned on his right side so that his back was almost but not quite touching the long bare warmth of her back and buttocks. He would, he decided, ignore the insistence of his bladder and try for another two hours' sleep.

Then, almost immediately, he was awake again and looking at the clock. 8:10 it said in those brisk, computerised numerals which implied so clearly their superiority to the cursive or Roman. They seemed to be saying "We are the last few years of the twentieth century and all is, technologically speaking, okay. Take it from us." He glanced again at Libby, almost as if to confirm her presence. She was still deeply asleep. He eased himself slowly out of bed and padded away down the hall to the bathroom. As he passed the chair by the bedroom door he felt an impulse to put on some clothes, his trousers at least had ended up on the chair, but decided against it. Central heating was definitely something he could get used to. And anyway, if she woke up now, or when he got back, it'd be a sight she'd be seeing more

of. That little paunch of his was not so very pronounc-
ed. Hadn't worried her last night, anyway. But he felt
nevertheless a ripple of shyness, of vulnerability, as he
walked away down to the bathroom, the carpet soft
against his soles, the only contact with anything other
than morning air.

The red floor tiles in the bathroom were colder but
not too cold. He pulled the door closed behind him. Lifting
the seat, he remembered with a smile the poem he'd
seen once in a feminist toilet which climaxed its long
remonstrance with the line "and after a piss they leave
the seat up". He sent a strong steam of urine into the
bowl, just left of the water to minimise the noise. In a
few minutes now, at the end of the passage, he'd be rummaging quietly in the kitchen and coming up with
breakfast. He glanced at the shelf in front of her mirror.
Although he must have seen them there at other times he
was surprised, pleasantly surprised, at the number of
shampoos, conditioners, moisturisers, the range of
balms and unguents she had there. For a no-nonsense
faminist Libby had her weak spots and Roy found it
almost consoling to think of the long line of women going back to Cleopatra and further who had sought to
improve, to dramatise, themselves in front of a mirror.
Men on the other hand, or the men he knew, had steered
pretty clear of it, refusing even signet rings and after-
shave. Sunlight soap and Ipana toothpaste. That was
about it, as far as Roy was concerned.

Yes, he'd decided, he'd just sneak up there to the kitchen
now and stir up some breakfast. Maybe just the toast
and coffee. Instant probably. A coffee grinder would wake
her for sure. Or maybe she'd be awake when he got
back to the bedroom for his underpants, in which case . . .

He gave his penis a final, careful shake and was just
moving across to the basin to wash his hands when the

whole bathroom filled with a sudden and silent explosion of light—and simultaneously an intense, though muffled heat. The light was so much like a flash of lightning, though golden and sustained, that Roy subconsciously started to count. But the heat that came with it was without precedent or comparison. The walls, he could feel with his whole body, were holding it out—but only just. He'd got to "three" when it all came clear. "Jesus," he yelled. "Hey, Libby." And rushed for the door which split as he reached it. In a last fragment of clarity he felt the weight of five collapsing storeys push his face into the tiles ... even as they, in turn, gave way beneath him.